SUSTAIN

A MURDEROUS CROWS ROCKSTAR ROMANCE

RHAPSODY
BOOK FIVE

AMY BOOKER

By

Amy Booker

AUTHOR'S NOTE

If you've read my previous books, you'll know the chapter names are all song titles. Music has been an integral part of my life and always sets the mood for my writing. Whether it's the overall energy of a song, the lyrics, or even the title, that tone carries through into my written words on the page. The playlist and a link can be found at the back of each book, or you can find them on my website: www.amybooker-author.com.

Life is not a dress rehearsal. You don't get a do-over. And no matter what happens, the show must go on.

CHAPTER 1

DEATH BY ROCK AND ROLL

MACKENZIE

"This was our compromise, remember Remy? You guys do this winter festival show in Aspen, and you get the holidays off. We can't back out now." The rhythm guitar player for Murderous Crows, the band I've managed for years, is suddenly trying to get out of this gig, and that is not going to fly with me.

"Yeah, but...Monroe..." he hedges.

I sigh. All of the guys in the band are now engaged, with Remy being the last to join the ranks, and all of a sudden, doing anything band-related has become a chore. Not necessarily Skyler, the drummer, and Logan, the bassist, since they're engaged to each other, but everyone else seems more focused on their relationships than the band.

And as someone who is married to her job, the

situation is starting to get annoying. The music used to always come first, and now it's like herding cats trying to get them all in one place at the same time to do anything.

"Monroe can come with you, Remy. You know this." I try super hard to not roll my eyes at how ridiculous it's getting with these guys.

"But she's got an exhibition starting soon. I told her I'd be around for support."

"Then you shouldn't have agreed to the Aspen gig," I say, biting the inside of my cheek so I don't say something I'll regret. "I'm sorry Remy, but the equipment arrived yesterday, and the crew is already there setting up. I'm about to head to the airport myself. And tickets have been sold out for months. We haven't canceled a show since we were living in Las Vegas, and I don't intend to start now."

Back in the early days, it wasn't unheard of for one of them to somehow screw up a gig in some way, and usually alcohol was involved. That all stopped the day our drummer Andy died in a drunk driving accident. Since then, everything has calmed down considerably. It wasn't exactly overnight for all of them, but the message eventually got through to get their shit together.

He's silent for a long time, and I get the sense there's more to it than he's saying. I don't get involved in the band's love lives, and don't intend on starting now, but for Remy to clam up like this is new. He's usually a pretty open book.

"Look, Remy, I know that you and Monroe haven't had the easiest time, but I thought since she moved to L.A. and you got engaged things were smooth sailing with you. Did something happen?"

"No, not at all. It's nothing like that," he says quickly.

"Then what is it?"

"It's just..."

Jesus Christ. "What is it, Remy? You can talk to me."

"You're going to think I sound like an idiot." His tone has changed, and now he almost sounds shy, which is not like him at all. Remy is the most outgoing and open of the band.

"I won't think you're an idiot. I promise." I sweep a loose strand of my stick-straight purple hair behind one ear and check the time on my digital watch. He's really cutting it close with this.

After another pause, he says, "I just don't want to leave her."

My cold heart instantly melts into a puddle on the floor, and I don't know how to respond. I've never had to deal with something like this. I stay far away from everyone's love lives on purpose. I don't want to become a topic of contention between any of them.

Unfortunately, my job puts me in the position of being the bad guy quite often. I'm used to it, but I don't always like it. Being the voice of reason around a bunch of creatives puts enough strain on us. Adding everyone's significant other's into the mix has only made times like this harder.

Lucky for all of them, I've never had a 'love life' to speak of to get in the way of the band's progress. 'Love' isn't a factor in my relationships. At least, not anymore.

The LA sunshine streams through my window, glinting off the platinum record I plan to present to the guys in Aspen. It's our first.

Our. Like I'm in the band...Oof

"Remy..."

"No, I know how stupid that sounds—"

"Not at all. In fact, that's probably the best reason you could have given to not want to go."

"But?"

"But we have a contract. We can't break it except for an act of God or something like that. We're committed." I'm sympathetic, but it doesn't change the facts. "I'm sorry, but we've got to do this festival. But I promise, you can take the first flight out when the concert is over. I won't make you do press or meet and greets afterward, okay?"

He's silent again, but I know he understands the deal. He's got a clear head about these things.

Usually.

Finally, he lets out a long breath. "Alright. Deal. I'll be there."

"I'll make a note that it's under protest."

"Thanks, Mac," he says, coming around to his normal self. "And thanks for not making fun of me."

"Never."

"See you tomorrow."

Such is the life of a rock 'n roll band manager. Putting out fires where there aren't any and looking for hidden infernos about to erupt. And Murderous Crows are known for throwing me curveballs every so often, like today.

Yay, me.

"So let me get this straight, Blackmore wants to consolidate artist management under one department?" I ask.

Eliza, the new Vice President of Blackmore Records nods. "With streaming revenues down and overhead high, yeah. They had Stratford come in and do an audit last month."

I wince. The fact that Blackmore used one of the most vicious consulting firms can only mean one thing: bloodletting.

"The board wants a 15% cut in operating costs. No exceptions for high-earners either, apparently." She gives me a pointed look. "Your whole team is on the chopping block, Ian."

My jaw tightens. We busted our asses to build the

artist recruitment program from the ground up. And now the fucking bean counters want it dismantled?

I scrub a hand over my face. "So if I say no..."

"Your position gets eliminated. Same severance as the others." Her gaze softens with sympathy. "I'm sorry. I know I'm putting you in an impossible spot. But I fought to have them offer you Chaos Fuel rather than just cut you loose."

The band's reputation flashes through my mind. Chaos is right. But unemployment is even less appealing.

The cold reality settles in my gut. My tidy world is about to transform into complete mayhem.

Band management was never really on my radar, but I've been involved in this industry in one way or another for a long enough time to know the ins and outs of it all. Hell, I bet I could run my own label if I wanted to.

My goal used to be keeping life somewhat predictable for my daughters back when we all called LA home. But after my ex-wife Brianna decided to return to England with the girls, my priorities shifted. We're originally from England but lived as dual citizens in LA after getting married. Trips back and forth between houses were the norm for us.

I'll admit I was pretty devastated when they left, the distance fucking hurt. It still does. But with my constant work travel as a talent scout, having them closer to my ex Brianna's family support system made sense. So I made the sacrifice.

They're still in the house we bought as a family near my hometown across the pond. And with my girls now an ocean away, I've embraced letting a little more chaos into my American life with my job being what it is.

Or was...

But Chaos Fuel? The band that can't seem to make headway on the charts, can't keep a bassist, and apparently can't keep a manager either, is suddenly about to become my next project. They're not exactly known as being easy to deal with.

I guess beggars can't be choosers.

If I want to stay with Blackmore, that is.

"So, who is going to find new artists if I accept?" There are only a handful of us currently scouting talent as it is.

"Troy and Rory will be taking that over."

"And what about Jan and Brett? What happens to them?" Things are clarifying themselves. Very sharply.

She silently lowers her gaze to the floor, and I know what that means. They're getting axed.

Holy shit. This is major.

My limited options start rotating in my mind. If I accept the new position, I can kiss my regular schedule goodbye. It will mean I will be on the road more than not, more than I am already, which means less time to visit my daughters. Until now, I could take regular

AMY BOOKER

flights back to England, and even work in some acquisition stops while in the U.K. But now this will mean my trips will entirely depend on the band.

I'm not so sure that's such a good thing.

"Your pay won't change," Eliza says sympathetically. "This isn't a demotion."

While that may be true, it's not exactly climbing the corporate ladder either. But then, I'm not the typical executive. After being in a band myself for years, I'd since gotten used to the predictability of a regular schedule. Now my whole life is going to be upended.

Maybe that *is* a good thing.

I've become a bit stagnant since the girls went back to England with their mother. This might shake things up a bit for me. Get the old juices flowing again.

Besides, I like a challenge. And Chaos Fuel is a challenge and a half. I'm the one that recruited them in the first place, so deep down I feel responsible for them anyway. This was probably inevitable. I know the guys, and I know what their general issues are, so it wouldn't be like I was going in blind.

But my girls...that's the only fly in the veritable ointment. Hayley and June are old enough to know I'm not around like I used to be as it is, six and five respectively, so where I am isn't really an issue. So long as I keep up our weekly video chats, it should be fine. I'll just try to visit them when I can. That's not much different from how it is now.

My heart aches at the thought of not seeing them in person as often as I can now, but again, my options are limited.

"Ian?" Eliza interrupts my internal war. "What do you think? If you're game, we've got a festival in Aspen coming up. It'll be a bit of trial by fire, but Mackenzie Roberts will be there with Murderous Crows to lend a hand if you need it. You know Mackenzie, right?"

My mind fills instantly with a vision of the talented and gorgeous band manager. We've known each other for years, and I even helped to sign Murderous Crows to the label not that long ago. Something inside me thrills at seeing her again. And the thought of working alongside her, at least for one festival, makes the offer all the more enticing.

"So, are you up for it?" Eliza asks again, anxious to get this problem resolved.

Settling the idea within myself, I resolve to at least try it out and see how it goes. I suppose if it doesn't work out, I can always do something else.

"Fine. Yeah. I'm up for it."

The narrator in my head: He was, in fact, not up for it.

I grew up in the desert. The Vegas desert. I am not equipped for snow. I'm just simply not built for it. But a weekend music festival in Aspen? For Murderous Crows, I can adjust. Managing their careers over the last decade and seeing them go from nobodies in local Vegas bars to now playing stadiums with a platinum record has been a meteoric rise that none of us were prepared for.

While all of the members now seem to have their shit together, for a long time they didn't, and I played babysitter more than manager. But after the fatal car accident, it's been a veritable love fest the last couple of years. Everyone has found a partner to share this crazy ride with.

I can feel all their eyes turn to me now.

Like I have time for a relationship.

Puh-leeze.

I barely have time for myself, let alone anyone else. My job has been the most important thing to me for a very long time. And I'm fucking good at it. I'm not going to let some guy with bedroom eyes sweep me off my feet only to end up barefoot in the kitchen raising our gaggle of kids.

Not that I have anything against kids. My best friend Chelsie and her husband Noah have two that I adore and just fawned all over when I was back in Vegas a few weeks ago. And maybe someday I'll be in a place in my life where kids make sense.

Just not now.

So, now I'm currently standing at the top of some mountain in Aspen, killing time before the band plays the music festival that starts downtown in a few days, freezing my ass off.

Our drummer, Skyler, said skiing is supposed to be relaxing. It's supposed to be fun.

We're on day two of this skiing thing. Yesterday was spent in a class with about ten other people and a ski instructor, Alexi, who was definitely nice to look at but made it difficult to concentrate on what he was teaching. He might be fun for a quick romp while I'm here. I'll have to look for him once we get back to the lodge...

The way he showed us yesterday, it seems easy enough. So long as the slope is relatively flat, and I can stop, I'm doing pretty good.

I might be a skier. Who knew?

But that was yesterday. Right now, we're looking down the mountain, and it doesn't look like the one we skied before at all. This one looks steep.

It looks like a goddamn Olympic run compared to the gentle incline we practiced on yesterday.

I turn to Skyler, eyes wide. "You've gotta be kidding me," I hiss under my breath. "That's a shear drop, not a hill!"

"You saw the same map I did. I think it's right."

We continue to watch people expertly jump off the lift and almost immediately start flying down the hill.

I swallow hard. "Okay. We got this. We took a lesson. We know the basics, right?"

"Right," she nods, more confidently than me.

Doubt and dread knot in the pit of my stomach. I've always prided myself on keeping everything tightly controlled. But staring down this mountain, I feel anything but in control.

Can I really do this? If I wipe out on this run, it won't just be some cute tumble I can laugh off over hot cocoa. We're talking broken bones or worse.

Just then, another skier whips past us, carving bold slashes into the pristine snow. Maybe I don't have to be bold. I just have to make it to the bottom intact. I take a deep breath of the cold mountain air and lower my goggles. The falling snow from the looming dark clouds above hits the lenses and melts.

Clenching my jaw, I shove any further doubts

aside. If I can conquer stadium tours and crisis PR for Murderous Crows, I can sure as hell handle a fucking ski slope.

"Let's do this, I guess," I say, pushing off with my knees shaking. I'm still sore from yesterday's adventure, but figure it'll ease up as I get back into it. Motioning for Skyler to go ahead of me I say, "After you."

"This was my idea, wasn't it..." she mutters as she pushes past me, easily gliding in a zig-zag pattern down the slope. She did pick up the instructions better than I did. But then, she was paying attention to what the hottie instructor was saying, not imagining what he'd look like in one of the saunas at our cheesy hotel.

I start after her and fall into the pattern of the movement. My knees are complaining slightly as I keep them bent and lean from side to side as I steer, but I'm doing okay for not having gone at this kind of speed before.

Skyler whoops loudly ahead, glancing over her shoulder at me. She's increasing her speed and her distance away, so I angle myself to go in a straighter line to try to keep up.

I definitely go faster than I was, but now the terrain is changing with more little bumps and hills popping up here and there. Whenever I approach one, my muscles tense up and I get a weird vertigo feeling like I'm going to fall, but somehow get through it.

If I had a steering wheel, I'd be white-knuckling it. As it is, I'm gripping my ski poles way too tightly.

Up ahead there's a hill that I'm not going to be able to avoid with my current pattern, so I lean in and brace myself for whatever is going to happen. Instead of wrecking in a pile of skis and poles, I actually do some sort of jump and land solidly. My skis are still facing forward, and I didn't fall on my ass.

In fact, I'm picking up even more speed.

This skiing thing is fucking amazing. I can totally do this.

That jump gave me more confidence and loosened me up to just go along with the terrain instead of trying to fight it. The cutting of the cold wind on my cheeks is exhilarating as I pick up even more speed.

The only issue I'm having now is the snow that's falling. It's almost a whiteout, and I can't see Skyler anymore. It's hard to see any distance in front of me at all, so I concentrate on what I can see, and notice another hill like the one I just jumped.

Preparing for it, I bend my knees further, anticipating the lift. But this time, it's not just a jump. I'm literally flying in the air.

That wasn't a hill. That was a fucking cliff.

I barely have time to register that the ground is coming up to meet me. For a split second, I think I'm going to be able to save it, but I don't land straight and start sliding sideways at speed. Before I can even think about adjusting my stance, my left ski catches on something, and I'm flying again.

I catch a flash of red coming at me fast through the blur of white. One of the lift poles. I try to twist away, but my skis catch again, and suddenly, it's on me.

My leg collides with unforgiving metal, and I swear I hear a sickening crack before I even feel it. Blinding pain shoots through my lower leg as it gives way.

I scream then, the sound going nowhere on the vacant slope. My cries mingle with the whipping wind as I crumble awkwardly into the snow.

The blizzard rages on, enveloping me in a haze of white. Through the cold powder swirling around me, I can see the lift pole, a red beacon now guiding me down into darkness.

I'm not an expert skier by any means, but when I see the woman who just passed me at an incredible rate of speed wipe out and slam right into the lift pole, I know they're most likely hurt, and I have to help. Maneuvering towards them, I eject out of my skis, stick them in an "X" shape in the snow so everyone else can steer clear, and rush over.

She's not moving.

Shit.

As I reach inside my ski vest for my phone, I kneel next to her and take off my gloves, feeling around her neck for a pulse. Thank god, there is one. Gently, I lift her goggles to see if she's conscious.

Holy hell. It's Mackenzie Roberts. The manager of Murderous Crows. Of course, she's in town for the music festival like I am.

"Mackenzie, can you hear me?" I tap her cheeks. "Mackenzie, wake up."

Nothing.

I dial the number for ski patrol rescue here at the resort listed on a sign attached to the pole, give them our location, and tell them a bit about what happened.

"Ian? Ian Summer?" Her voice is soft but cuts through my rising anxiety.

"I'm here," I say, turning my full attention to her. "Rescue is on the way. What hurts?"

"Everything," she groans, still not moving. That worries the shit out of me.

"Can you move at all?" I ask, and as her brow furrows at that, I say, "Only if you can. If it hurts, don't move."

"My leg," her brow creases more. "I think it's broken."

"Okay, then don't move. They'll be here soon." I notice her start to shiver and realize she's basically lying in the snow. Even the best ski gear isn't made for long direct contact with the cold. Taking off my coat, I place it over her and tuck it around her carefully. "Anything else hurt? Or just the leg?"

Her face scrunches up in pain, and her breathing turns into sharp little breaths. She lifts an arm to cover her eyes, hiding her emotion from me.

"*Fuck*," she snarls through gritted teeth.

I pull her arm away from her face, revealing her stunning violet eyes that are only a few shades lighter than the wisps of purple hair peaking out from her wool cap. "Hey, if ever there was a time to cry, this would be it. I promise I won't tell anyone. Your badass rep is safe with me."

She lets out a primal scream from somewhere deep in her gut that tries to echo across the mountain but is dampened by the heavy surrounding snowfall.

"Or, you know. You could scream, too."

Then the tears start, but she's quick to wipe them away. "Sorry. It just *fucking hurts*."

"Give me your hand," I say, offering mine to her, and she takes it hesitantly with a questioning look. "When it gets to be too much, squeeze my hand as hard as you need to. I can take it."

No sooner do I say that than Mackenzie clutches my hand so tightly my breath catches in my throat. I wasn't expecting her to take me up on the offer so soon or with so much vigor.

She's fucking strong.

"Did you know that while men are typically stronger, women have much better stamina, and can exercise for around seventy-five percent longer?" I ask, trying to distract her from the pain that's radiating through her. It's completely random and should throw her off.

"What the fuck?" she asks, her grip on my hand lessening. "Where did that come from? Actually, what are you doing here? I didn't know any execs from Blackmore were going to be here. *Ahhh*," she hisses, pulling in air through her teeth as a wave of pain hits.

At least my tactic worked, and she doesn't look like she's going to fold within herself any longer.

"Oh, so you didn't hear that I've been 'volunteered' to manage Chaos Fuel, then?"

She scoffs, but then winces and sucks in another breath. The vice around my hand tightens again. "Volunteered?" she chokes out.

"Yeah. Lucky me, eh?" I can't help but chuckle, even though the snowstorm around us seems to be increasing by the minute, making me worry about more than just Mackenzie's leg.

"To be fair, Ron was kind of a dick. He was a half-ass manager too."

I nod my head to the side. She's not wrong. Still, I had no intentions of getting into band management.

"Too true," I say. "But that left things in a bad spot. So, here I am."

"Lucky me," she whispers, and I'm not sure she meant for me to hear her. Or, whether it was a good or bad thing.

Just then, the sound of a motor of some kind comes from behind me. I turn to see the ski patrol snowmobile and stand to wave them over.

"Shit. Skyler's going to freak out when she sees I'm not behind her," Mackenzie says, anxiety now rising again.

I immediately go back into rescue mode and kneel

beside her, taking her hand again. "I'll call her and let her know."

"Wait, aren't you going to come with me?" The worry in her eyes edged with her pain, tugs at me. I can't *not* go with her.

"Of course. I'll go with you." I give her a reassuring smile. "But they're going to tend to you for a bit before we get moving, so I can call her now."

Mackenzie Roberts is not one to ask for help or assistance of any kind. Not unless she really needs it. So, for her to ask me to go with her for medical treatment means she's *really* hurting.

She gives me her phone, and I start calling people as she directs me and leave messages for others while the rescuers administer first aid and get her secured for transport down the mountain.

"We've actually closed the mountain," one of the rescue crew says, squinting up into the squall surrounding us. "This snow came in way quicker than it was supposed to."

"Oh?" I ask. Surprised that the weather here can be this unpredictable.

"Yup. We can figure out a lot of things pretty accurately. I mean, it *is* science. But Mother Nature has a mind of her own sometimes."

"How bad is it going to get?" I ask, now worried about our current situation, and if we'll be able to get down the mountain safely.

"Pretty bad."

Great.

I scan the slope around us, taking in the whiteout conditions. The wind lashes at us now, biting any exposed skin. It'd be all too easy to lose your way in this, for the cold to leach away body heat distressingly fast.

My gaze settles on Mackenzie, taking in her pale, drawn face. If transporting her was risky before, it's infinitely more precarious now. And that's not even considering how we'll make it back to our lodgings in this blizzard.

My stomach sinks, scenarios flashing. If we get stranded out here, Mackenzie's leg break could turn life-threatening fast. I force myself to exhale, nodding to the squad.

"Right then. We'd best get moving."

The sooner we get off this peak, the better our chances if this storm hits full force. I just hope we beat the worst of it in time. Mackenzie's faced enough peril already today without that.

The patrol squad swarms around Mackenzie, movements urgent but precise. One medic begins cutting away her ski pant leg to expose the injury while another prepares an inflatable splint. I avert my eyes as fabric tears, not wanting to infringe on her privacy.

The medics work wordlessly, communicating through loaded glances and terse gestures. A neck brace is settled despite Mackenzie's protests. They

slide an insulation pad underneath before immobi-
lizing her entire leg under the hardened splint.

"That should hold it for transport," the lead medic
confirms, and I see Mackenzie exhale in relief

I catch the hints of purple mottling and swelling
distorting her limb where they cut away the pant leg.
Bile burns the back of my throat. I squeeze her hand,
wishing I could erase the trauma, both sustained and
yet to come.

"Who the hell thought it was a good idea to attach
slippery sticks to the bottom of your feet so you could
slide down a fucking mountain?" Mackenzie is griping
to anyone who will listen as they carefully maneuver
her onto the litter. "I mean, really. It's stupid."

Without disagreeing, I grab my slippery sticks,
attach them to the bottoms of my feet, and slide down
the mountain along with the rescue crew to the
medical center.

*Note to self: Buy Mackenzie a shirt that says, 'I'm with
stupid.'*

P ain I can handle. Even excruciating pain like I'm in now as they finish the x-rays on my leg in the resort medical center. However, I don't do humiliation. It's not in my repertoire of things I know how to deal with. My typical way of dealing with heavy emotions is either to get angry and tough it out while lashing out at the world or just the opposite - completely shutting down.

I haven't been in a situation like this in a long time: having to deal with something major in front of someone important. Not that Ian is super important to me, but he is a pretty big deal at the label, and for me to just wipe out like that in front of him, *and* to have him basically rescue me is something I'm never going to be able to live down. Not within myself, anyway.

I am a smart woman. My friend Chelsie constantly

tells me that I should be in MENSA, or be a doctor or something, but I don't have patience for pretentious bullshit. That especially applies when it comes to guys. And especially musicians, or former musicians for that matter. So, I should know better than to get all worked up over Ian Summer. Besides, I think he's married.

He's the former lead singer of the band Corpse Limousine, and how he fell into the business side of things I have no idea. We've met several times over the years, but seeing him still sitting in the exam room after coming back from getting X-rays makes my heart skip a few beats.

"You're still here, huh?" I ask, not sure how I feel about any of this. It's one thing to rescue me in the moment, and a completely other thing to hang out while I get put back together. It's above and beyond, and unexpected. "You don't have to stick around. I'll find my way back to my hotel."

His green eyes crinkle as he smiles. He's almost a different person when he does. Not that he's ugly when he doesn't, I've just never seen such a transformation with a smile. It's devastating when the full effect of it is pointed at you. And his shaggy light brown hair that makes me want to run my fingers through it isn't helping matters at all. If I was standing and my leg wasn't splinted, my knees would totally be weak right now.

"You trying to get rid of me?" he chuckles. "You're

going to have to do better than that." He gets up to help me get settled while we wait for results. "What can I get for you? Something hot to drink? Another blanket? Your lips still look a little blue…"

He's such a worry wort. I never would have pegged him as the caretaker type. He always seemed a bit indifferent about anything and anyone around him. To see him so attentive to me is just weird.

"No. I'm fine. Really. Thanks though."

This earns me a narrow-eyed squint of disbelief. "You're a horrible liar, Mac." He shoves his fists into his pockets, suddenly awkward. "I'm starting to feel a bit helpless here."

"And I'm trying really hard to feel bad for you."

"I can tell." The smile is back, and I instantly feel a little bit better.

Sarcastic banter, I can do. And it is helping. Whether he knows it or not, just having him here with me is comforting.

"Thank you," I say, serious for a change. I think the pain meds are kicking in. I'm feeling a bit sappy all of a sudden.

"For what?" He seems surprised that I would be grateful.

Now I'm not sure if I should be offended. "Everything. I don't know what I would have done if you weren't there."

He nods, "Well, that was lucky, yes." His cheeks redden a little, and my stomach does a small flip at the sight of it. "I'm just glad I was there and able to help. It was quite a crash."

A silence falls heavily and awkwardly between us.

It's a well-known fact around the world I'm sure, that I don't know how to flirt. I don't flirt because I don't know how. Plain and simple. My attraction to people is usually a cerebral thing, not a stomach-flipping kind of thing. If someone can keep up with me in an intelligent conversation, and hold their own, that is hella sexy to me. I'm not usually swayed by the combination of a sexy smile and a to-die-for British accent.

This is new.

That's not to say Ian isn't intelligent. Quite the opposite. Whenever we've seen each other in the past, bantering with him has always been fun. But for some reason, today, right now, there seems to be an undercurrent of some kind flowing between us that I don't recognize. I've never felt something like this before with anyone.

It suddenly strikes me that he's the whole package. I've never seen the whole package in person.

And, wow, I'm getting ahead of myself. It must be the pain meds making my brain go wonky. I'll need to be careful around him, or I'll say something I'll end up regretting when I have a clearer head.

"Mackenzie?" Ian's voice slices through my internal thoughts. "If you keep staring at me like that, I'm afraid I'll start blushing."

"You're already blushing," I say without thinking.

Fuck. Mackenzie, what the hell?

That makes the flush in his cheeks deepen even further, and he looks a little tongue-tied.

"Shit, sorry," I say quickly, wishing desperately I'd be able to pull the words back from the air between us. As I attempt to sit up, a flash of pain shoots through my leg and up into my hip, causing me to cry out.

Ian immediately is at my side, hands on my shoulders, easing me back into the pillows.

"No, no," he says gently. "You're perfectly right. I am a bit flush. It's unnaturally warm in here, don't you think?"

I stare at him for a second, not sure how I want to play this. Do I go along with this obvious lie and deflection? Or call him out on it since I happen to feel the same?

Remembering that I'm on heavy pain medication, I side with the lie. Who knows what a clear head would think?

"It is very warm in here," I say, avoiding his gaze. It's already been established I'm a horrible liar, but we need a release valve on this conversation. "Sorry, whatever is in that juice box they're pumping through my veins is making me a little loopy." I look up at the IV bag hanging on a pole beside the bed, mostly to avoid his gaze on me.

We're both stuck in some staring/avoiding contest that feels like cat and mouse, and we keep changing places. I must admit, it's kind of thrilling.

And I need to stop this. Right now. I can't pursue anything with Ian. Especially at a work event. It would be completely unprofessional.

"Speaking of work..." I start, sneaking a glance at him.

"Were we?" His eyes shine with mischief. It's fucking adorable.

Stop it.

"No, but we probably should," I risk another look up at him. Damnit, he's smiling. "Are all of your guys here?"

He nods. "Yes, they got in last night. Late, as always, but they made it. What about your flock? All present and accounted for?"

"Same. They came in last night too." My brow furrows as it dawns on me that I'll need to work through this festival with an injury. I'm positive my leg is broken, which is going to make getting around, especially in the snow, a nightmare. I don't know that I can do it.

Suddenly I'm overwhelmed, and everything hits me at once. My eyes start tearing up again, and I quickly bury my face in my hands to hide my crying from Ian.

The level of unprofessionalism I've been displaying is outrageous.

"Hey, hey," he says, sliding an arm around my shoulder and pulling me into him. His spicy cologne pierces my senses and makes me feel instantly comforted. "I get it. You're worried about being able to work the festival. Don't worry about a thing. I'll help take care of everything."

It's then that the enormity of my predicament really washes over me. This isn't just about working the festival. I'm going to be at the mercy of any and all help I can get to even function. There's no way I could ask Ian to help with all of that.

The tears increase in voracity, and I can feel my shoulders shake. I wish desperately my best friend, Chelsie, was here. She'd know how to help and do it without being asked.

Ian kisses the top of my head and pulls me tighter against him, and I don't fight it. Before this, we've only been physical in a friendly way – genial hugs hello and goodbye at events, playful slaps on the shoulder or arm. I think we may have even done the handshake and peck on the cheek.

This is different. This is new.

This is *nice*.

"I've got you. Don't worry. I've got you," he whispers into my hair.

Goosebumps run all over me. I've never heard those words spoken to me before. *Ever*.

I'm not someone you typically speak those words to.

Or am I?

CHAPTER 6

HONEY DON'T THINK

IAN

The sudden instinct to want to protect Mackenzie and take care of her is surprising. I'm not a touchy-feely kind of guy, so wrapping myself around her like this is entirely out of character for me. That is, apart from my daughters, June and Hayley. They get all the hugs I can manage when I see them, which isn't as often as I'd like.

Knowing that Mackenzie isn't the type to ever ask for help makes me want to do it even more. I understand what it's like to be too stubborn for your own good because I'm just like her in that regard. And I think if I were in her situation, deep down, I'd want someone to step up and take care of me.

I'd grumble and whinge about it endlessly, but secretly, I'd probably like being tended to. Especially if it was by Mackenzie. I haven't had enough of that in my life, especially since my divorce.

As soon as I think that, I pull out and wave my own inner red flag. I can't be thinking about Mackenzie in any way other than professionally. Yes, this is an extenuating circumstance, but once this passes, it's back to business as usual. The keyword is 'business.'

A doctor enters the room, and for a moment, I can feel Mackenzie tense next to me. I'm not sure if it's because I'm sitting on the bed with her and someone walked in or if she's worried about what the doctor's about to say. On the off chance that it's me she's tense about, I stand up, releasing her, and I suddenly feel like I want to jump back in and hold her again. Shield her from whatever this guy's about to say. But, I restrain myself.

"Well, you took quite a spill, huh, Ms. Roberts?" The doctor says. Not really asking a question.

Mackenzie just stares at him, her eyes still shiny, but a determination in her expression to handle whatever comes at her in the next few moments. Again, I want to hold her hand or something. I feel like a bystander, which, I guess I am.

"Right..." the doctor continues after not getting the jovial response he was probably expecting. "Well, there's definitely a break, but it's not as bad as it could have been. You were extremely lucky." He slides the X-ray over the light box and turns it on.

"I don't feel very lucky," Mackenzie mutters,

crossing her arms over her chest. I smile inwardly, recognizing the tenacious spirit is back in her demeanor.

"Well, you only fractured your fibula, the bone on the outside of your calf, and not your tibia, which is the bigger, weight-bearing shinbone. Plus it's just a hairline fracture. So, we won't have to do a full-blown cast. But, you're going to have one hell of a bruise for sure."

"Does that mean I'll be able to walk?" Mackenzie asks, not even looking at the X-ray. She just wants the bottom line. Typical Mackenzie.

"I wouldn't recommend it in the short term," the doctor says, taking off his glasses, and wiping them on the hem of his scrubs shirt. "I assume you don't live in the area?"

"No, I'm just here for the festival," she says impatiently. Her eyes are starting to fill again, and I think it's more out of frustration than anything else at this point. "So, what *can* I do?"

He stares at her for a moment, gauging how he'll respond. He seems to realize the kind of person he's dealing with in Mackenzie.

No nonsense.

"You'll have to wear a brace, which we'll fit you with. The fibula is a stabilizing bone, so we'll need to shore that up for a while." He pulls the X-ray from the light box and shuts it off. "You'll probably be in the acute pain stage for at least a day or two, and we'll give you medicine to get through that. You'll need to check in with your regular doctor once you get home and, most likely, an orthopedist--"

"Wait, no narcotics." She suddenly declares adamantly as she sits up and twists to look up at the IV bag, squinting to read the label.

The doctor and I both glance at each other in surprise. I shrug, knowing absolutely nothing about Mackenzie's medical history.

"Is there an allergy or... An issue that I should know about?" the doctor asks, eyebrows raising in concern. He takes a few cautious steps toward the IV, already flooding morphine into her system.

"What? No. Nothing like that," she says, shaking her head. Her expression appears confused and haunted, and my curiosity is piqued. "I just don't like being out of it. I don't want to take anything that could be...I just don't want any."

He nods to himself, understanding, though I wish he could explain it to me. I would think she would want to be pain-free if possible. Plus, she knows she's been getting narcotics already in her IV. This sudden shift is a bit confusing.

"Can we keep the IV going for now, and when we release you in the next couple of hours, we'll go over your pain management plan? I think the risk outweighs the reward to your pain level for a little while at least. You are going to be hurting."

She studies him for a long moment, and even I

begin to squirm under the intensity of it. Eventually, she nods and sits back, pushing into her pillows with her eyes closed, releasing a deep breath.

I glance up at the doctor expectantly, unsure of what's next. I'm not a big fan of hospitals, and seeing as Mackenzie's injury isn't as bad as originally thought, I'm anxious to get us out of here.

He nods at us as he leaves the room. "We'll be back in shortly with the brace and more instructions. Just sit tight."

Once he's gone there's a heavy silence between us. I'm unsure if I should bring up what just happened, or let it go. Changing the subject feels just as awkward as saying something.

"Sorry, I just..." Mackenzie whispers, avoiding eye contact with me.

I hold my hands up. "You don't owe me or anyone an explanation. It's completely up to you what course of treatment you take. Hell, you could jump out of that bed right now and run out of here, and I wouldn't stop you."

That at least gets a smirk from her. "Really?" The dubious glance she gives me is worth it.

"Well, I might at least call after you."

"Is that all?" I love the sparkle of challenge in her eyes.

"To be honest, I don't think you'd get very far," I smirk right back. "You know, broken leg and all."

"Yeah, there is that." Her brow creases, and she's suddenly serious again.

"What is it?" I ask.

She glances up at me, reluctant to voice whatever it is that's bothering her. "I don't know how I'm going to navigate this festival if I can't get around. You've seen me at shows, Ian. I'm never in the same spot for more than a minute. This is going to be a nightmare."

It's true. I've seen Mackenzie in action at a few Murderous Crows shows, and she's constantly moving. A broken leg is going to be a severe hindrance, especially with all the snow that's currently falling.

"Well, lucky for you that I'm here then. I'll just handle everything for both of our bands. It won't be a problem."

How hard could it be? Most of the preparations are already made for all of us. It's just a matter of getting everyone in the right place at the right time.

Nine rockstars. No problem. I have two young girls. I can handle some adults.

The dubious glare now coming from Mackenzie is almost laughable. The morphine must really be kicking in now since the glassiness in her gaze isn't tears anymore.

"Do you have my phone?" she asks. "Can I have it, please?" She holds a hand out expectantly.

"No."

She narrows her eyes at me. "What do you mean, no? Did you leave it on the mountain?"

"No, it's not on the mountain." I can't help the smile that cracks through my attempt at being stern.

She's not amused.

"Give me my phone, Ian."

I'm almost tempted to give in and hand it over, but I hold my ground. She just broke her bloody leg, and she's on morphine. There's no way I'm letting her try to conduct business right now.

"You need to rest," I say, reaching over and plumping her pillows behind her. "I told you, I'll handle everything. Don't worry."

I catch a twitch of her lips before it turns into a scowl. "I'm not a baby," she mutters.

"Nobody said you were," I sigh, sitting next to her on the bed again and draping an arm around her as she leans her head on my shoulder. "In fact, I think you're a talented business person, and very good at your job. You're just getting sidelined for this game, that's all."

"Very good?" she asks, glaring up at me. I'd worry if the smirk wasn't back along with it. "You think I'm just 'very good' at my job? Do you know how hard I work? I do the job of three managers – the tour manager, the band manager, the production manager-_"

"That's what you heard out of everything I said? Sorry. Sorry. I meant to say 'best.' You're the absolute best in the business. Hands down." She nods and leans further into me. "Geesh, overachiever."

"I heard that."

"I know you did," I smile.

When I came to Aspen, I thought I'd get a few runs on the slopes, some Scotch by the fire in the lodge, and dive headfirst into the new manager gig.

I didn't expect this. I didn't expect this at all.

Another note to self: The old adage is true – When you least expect it – expect it.

I guess it's a good thing I'm on morphine right now. Otherwise, I'd be freaking the fuck out trying to figure out how I'm going to do my job when I can't easily get around.

This is my worst nightmare.

A huge festival featuring the biggest acts in the business, and I'm benched. I'm not entirely helpless, but the blizzard just made my job a million times harder than it needs to be. Ian holding my phone hostage isn't helping either.

I must fall asleep with my head on Ian's shoulder, because the next thing I know, there's another doctor in the room with a leg brace. When I move to sit up, pain shoots down my leg. I'd almost forgotten it was broken. I'm surprised I was able to fall asleep with all the adrenaline coursing through me.

Maybe that's what happened. I finally crashed.

Ha. Literally.

"What's so funny?" Ian asks, getting up from the side of the bed and shaking out his arm. I'm guessing it must have fallen asleep while he was holding me.

It's then that I notice how much I liked it when he held me. How safe I felt in his arms. Safe enough to fall asleep, at least. That's new. I also notice he's not wearing a wedding ring anymore. I could have sworn he was married.

"Huh? Oh, nothing," I say, shaking my head and trying to clear the cobwebs. Unfortunately, pain medicine makes me chatty, and I have no filter. "What happened to your wedding ring? I thought you were married."

I need to shut the hell up.

The doctor holding my brace looks at me, then looks at Ian questioningly. He's apparently invested in the unfolding drama in front of him more than he is taking care of my leg. Fair enough.

Ian looks down at his hand as if to double-check that what I've said is true, and his brow furrows slightly. If I had to guess, I'd say the hurt that flashed behind his eyes for a second has a story behind it.

"I was," he says, suddenly stoic. "I'm not anymore."

I stare at his hand as he shoves it back into his pocket, wanting to know the story. In all of our meetings, we've never really talked about personal lives. It's always been about business or the industry. I appreciated that about him. But now I'm curious. Something tells me getting him to talk about it won't be easy. I should probably leave it alone.

The new doctor goes through putting the brace on and gives me instructions on how to use and care for it. It seems simple enough. I'll also be getting crutches to use for the first few days or so. I really did luck out, considering how bad this could have been.

We're barely done talking about follow-up care when the first doctor comes back. I didn't catch anybody's names. Though, I don't think I'd be able to remember anyway. It's hard enough to pay attention to my care instructions.

"Where are you two staying?" He asks, looking between the two of us.

"Oh, we're not together," Ian and I say at the same time. We were both awfully fast to dispel the notion that we'd be a couple. I look over at him to find him looking at me, and when our eyes meet, a jolt goes through me, making me feel like what I just said was a lie.

We both quickly turn back to the doctor.

Odd.

"Oh, my mistake," the doctor says, cheeks flushing. "I just thought since... Never mind. The reason I ask is because almost all the roads are closing now, and the worst of the storm hasn't even hit yet. You might be stuck here."

My throat tightens, and my heart starts to race. I don't want to be here any longer than I have to.

"I'm staying at the hotel way over near the airport," I say, knowing almost instantly that it's probably too far for me to get to. "There isn't Uber or Lyft? Or something like that?"

The doctor shakes his head. "Unfortunately, even rideshare or taxis are going to be near impossible to find now. Besides, you wouldn't want to be on the roads in these conditions. We're all getting ready to hunker down for a few days."

"Days?" Ian and I ask in unison again, but this time we don't look at each other. The thought of being stuck here for another hour, let alone days, makes my stomach clench. Ian must be just as reluctant as I am about it, and I feel bad that I've put him in this position.

"It happens more than you'd think," the doctor continues. "Tell you what, though. If you can find yourself a way out of here, I'm happy to release you. So long as you promise me you have someone to look after you." He eyes Ian as he says this, and flashes a devilish smile before leaving.

The silence in the room once he's gone is deafening. Things were already starting to get awkward between Ian and me before the 'getting stranded' topic even came up. Now it's even worse.

"Let me make a few calls," Ian says briskly without looking back as he walks out.

I watch as he goes, still in a bit of a daze at the entire situation. Forty-eight hours ago, I was snug and comfy in my LA apartment with a glass of red wine while video chatting with my best friend Chelsie. Now that seems like years ago. So much has happened since then.

My life has always happened fast. I barely have time to hold onto anything before the next thing is thrown at me, and the next destination is pinned. If I'm not planning the next level of success, I'm cleaning up the messes everyone else leaves behind. This broken leg is going to cause so many more problems. I can already feel my skin itch with the urge to start fixing things that haven't even happened yet.

Before I can get too far down the rabbit hole that is my brain, Ian comes rushing back into the room, and he has one of my rescue team with him.

"Hey, so this is Billy. He's got a snowcat and has very kindly offered to take us to my cabin, which isn't that far from here."

He speaks so quickly that I can barely keep up with what he says.

"You have a cabin?"

He pulls up and gives me an odd look. "Again, that's what you took from that sentence?"

I think about it for a second, then turn to the medic, a stout older man with a white beard. He'd make a perfect department store Santa Claus. "Hi, Billy. Thank you for the ride offer."

"No problem," he says, glancing between Ian and me. "Happy to help."

I'm about to ask if Billy can give me a ride to my hotel, but Ian starts talking before I can get the words out.

"No, he can't take you to your hotel. I already asked." He pats Billy's shoulder.

"Sorry, I've got to get to my daughter's house before the storm settles in," Billy says apologetically. "But if we're able to leave shortly, I can at least get you folks out of here and somewhere more comfortable."

"Right. Let me go find that doctor about a release," Ian says, heading out of the room again.

"I should go warm up the snowcat," Billy says, putting his bright red woolen cap back on. "I'll see you in a little bit."

And, I'm suddenly left alone again. Things are at least happening, but they're happening *without* me. I don't like this feeling.

I'm not in control of anything.

A fter carrying Mackenzie inside the cabin and planting her safely on the couch, I run back out to the snowcat and grab her crutches.

"You two stay safe," Billy says with a smile. "These storms can be unpredictable. You've got my number now if you need anything."

I nod and give a wave as I shut the cab door. I only hesitate for a moment to watch what, for all intents and purposes, is a mini tank, roll on its treads into the darkening squall.

Shutting the door to the cabin behind me, I stomp and shake the snow from my person and kick off my boots, glad to be out of the frigid cold.

"Did we really just hitch a ride with Santa Claus?" Mackenzie asks from across the room. I can hear in her voice that she's still a little loopy from the morphine.

"Indeed, we did," I say, searching for the remote for the fireplace. It's warm in here from the furnace, but not as warm as I'd like. "Didn't you see that bag of toys he had behind his seat, or Rudolph leading us here?"

"I wondered what that was," she laughs. "I thought it might be a body."

"A body?" I ask, glancing over to her to see if she's okay.

"Yeah..." she furrows her brow as if concerned about herself now, too. "Sorry, I hang out with the guys too much. They watch a lot of horror films."

"Ah," I nod my understanding. It makes sense.

"What are you looking for?" she asks, her laugh dying down.

"The bloody remote for the fireplace. I don't see it anywhere."

She bursts out in laughter again, and now I know for sure that she's lost it.

"What?" I ask, genuinely concerned for her mental state. "What's so funny?"

She points to the side of the large fireplace that takes up half of the back wall of the large cabin.

"See all that?" she asks, waving her hand slowly up and down. "That's called firewood. We use that here in America to build fires."

It's only then that I see the cord of wood stacked against the side of the rock fireplace. I can't help the chuckle that bubbles up as I feel my face heat.

Fucking hell.

"In my defense, my fireplace at home is gas and uses a remote. And, I haven't spent a lot of time here yet." I head over to the wood pile and start constructing a fire. "I happen to also be American, just so you know. Dual citizenship."

"Oh, really? When did you convert?"

A snort escapes me before I can control it. I glance over my shoulder at her to give a snarky reply and see her struggling to shrug out of her ski jacket. *Shit. I should have got her settled first.*

"Damn. Forgive me. I should have made you comfortable before running around trying to do everything else." I rush over and help her out of her coat, and as she leans back, I prop her bad leg under a pile of throw pillows. She only flinches once. "Better? What else can I get you? Hot cocoa? Tea?"

"You can stuff your tea," she says, pulling the throw blanket I place over her up to her chin as she closes her eyes. "I'll take some of the first thing."

"Hot cocoa?"

"Yes, please." Her voice drifts off, and I think she might be falling asleep again. The pain medicine sure does knock her out.

I head into the kitchen area and start rummaging through the cabinets. I was hoping to find some instant hot cocoa packets, but don't find any. The couple I rented this place from last minute said the cabin was stocked, which, for the most part, it is. Just no cocoa.

Standing in the middle of the room, staring at the flickering reflection of the firelight on the copper pans hanging above the island, I scratch my head. My eye catches on the gift basket left as a 'welcome' present or something for me. More like a *'Thanks for overpaying for your stay,'* gift. Sifting through the items, I find what I was looking for: A stack of dark chocolate bars. *Perfect.*

I warm up some milk in a pot on the stove as I break one of the bars into small pieces, and once the milk is steaming, I lower the heat and add the chocolate, stirring it constantly. I'm instantly transported back to when my mother used to make this for me on cold London afternoons after coming in from sledding on a hill down the road with my friends.

I guess winter sports have always kind of been my thing.

I send some quick texts to make sure all is well at the hotel, and once the cocoa is ready, I pour it into mugs and head back into the main room. Mackenzie did fall asleep, so I stoke the fire in the fireplace and sit back next to her. While I did try to be careful not to wake her, she opens her eyes and squints into the fire for a minute.

"You okay?" I ask, gently pushing a lock of her hair out of her eyes. "I made hot cocoa for you."

She wakes in earnest then and holds her hands out

in a grabby motion. Taking the mug from me, she wraps her fingers around it and breathes in the steam. "This smells amazing."

"I'll pass on your compliments to my mother. It's her recipe," I smile, still a little nostalgic for my care-free childhood.

Her mug halts halfway to her lips, and her eyes widen. "Wait, this isn't packaged hot chocolate?"

I shake my head. "Nope. Made with my own two hands."

"Holy shit. Marry me." She clamps a hand over her mouth as I raise an eyebrow at her. "I didn't...I mean--"

"Did you just propose to me, Mackenzie?" I ask, pretending to be serious. "Don't you think it's just a tad premature? I mean, I've known you for a while, but..."

Her face has gone beet red, and it's extremely difficult for me to hold in my laughter. "I didn't mean that, for real. Obviously. It was just a saying."

I crease my brows in mock confusion. "Hmm. As you've so kindly pointed out, I'm not originally from here, so is that an "American" saying? You just go around asking people to marry you? Odd tradition." I make sure to use air quotes to rile her up even more.

She finally catches on that I'm messing with her, but she's still embarrassed.

"Oh my god, fuck off," she says, blowing on her

cocoa. A grin finds its way and breaks through. It's beautiful.

Actually, in the warm firelight of the room, everything about her is beautiful. She seems to glow, despite everything she's been through today. Before, I thought it was just her kinetic energy since she's always on the go, always getting things done. I never stopped to really *look* at her.

And she's stunning.

Between her long amethyst hair, wide violet eyes, and that damn sharp sense of humor and intelligence, it's impossible not to notice her beauty. I feel as if I've caught some sort of mystical being from the fae wild, and am the first person to see her true nature.

"Earth to Ian," I hear her call my name, and it snaps me out of my reverie, but I'm still staring at her.

I quickly avert my gaze to the fire and clear my throat. "Sorry, I zoned out for a minute there. Did you say something?"

She eyes me curiously for a second. "I said to definitely give my compliments to your mother. This is amazing."

"Oh, of course," I say and shift a bit uncomfortably. "I'll tell her." What I don't say is that my mother and I haven't exactly gotten along since my divorce from Brianna. But then, my mother hasn't understood many of my life choices; the band, moving to America, any of it. I'm an enigma to her. Always have been.

My awkward response earns me another odd look

from Mackenzie, but she doesn't press me on it, and I'm grateful. The last thing I want to do right now is discuss my mother. Though, to be fair, I did mention her first.

"So, how did you snag this winter palace while the rest of us had to book the no-tell motel by the airport?" She sounds annoyed, and rightfully so. It does appear as though I've gotten special treatment with my lodging.

"Well, as mentioned, I was a last-minute addition to the entourage, and Ron's room was already given away. So, I offered to get my own accommodation. And, well," I hold a sweeping arm out, "who wouldn't choose this if they could?"

She arches an eyebrow at me, and I have to look away before I get lost staring at her again.

"But, mi casa es tu casa, as it were," I say, glancing out the windows at the snowstorm raging outside. "It looks like you're stuck roughing it here with me for tonight at least."

Something charged stirs in the air between us, and neither of us says anything else about her having to stay the night with me.

And now, it's all I can think about.

Fuck.

I really wish the awkwardness that just landed between us wasn't there. Things were going so well before I went and made it weird by asking him to marry me.

What the fuck was that?

I'm still not feeling any pain, thanks to the residual morphine from the IV I had. Unless I move, then I really feel it all the way up to my hip. So, it looks like I'll be stuck in this position on the couch for the foreseeable future.

"Is there anything else I can get you?" Ian asks in a gentle voice. "Are you hungry?"

I roll my eyes. "Don't tell me you cook too. I may propose again."

He chuckles, his chest shaking with laughter. "Ok, I won't tell you then."

I sip my cocoa, keeping my gaze fixed on the fire. I can't help my own smile, though. "Of course, you do."

"Now, what does that mean?" he asks, feigning defensiveness. "You just told me not to tell you. What's a poor cooking sod to do?"

His smile catches me off guard again as I glance at him. He really is too perfect. From what I know of him, anyway. Which isn't much.

We met several years ago at the Raven in Las Vegas when Murderous Crows were still nobodies. Ian was instrumental in getting them signed along with Eliza Kerr, one of the major label executives. It was a long process with Blackmore, since the band kept fucking up showcases, and singer Jake's getting arrested and wrongfully charged for then drummer Andy's death in a tragic car accident. It hasn't been an easy road to get where we are. But we wouldn't be here at all if Ian didn't believe in them, in us. He's been one of our biggest cheerleaders.

We owe him a lot.

As he sighs heavily and stares into the fire, I take advantage of the chance to examine him a little closer. With his knowledge of the music industry, I've always found him attractive. He's always good for a stimulating conversation. And he seems to be ready with a joke or something to lighten the mood whenever things get too heavy.

Like in the hospital.

If he wasn't there to lift my mood, I might have

spiraled with anxiety. But he was calm and cool-headed in an emergency. I don't know what I would have done if he hadn't stopped on the slope and saved me, either. For all I know I could still be on that mountain, freezing to death. I was extremely lucky he was there.

"Thank you," I say, but it comes out as a whisper.

He gives me an odd look. "You don't have to keep thanking me for the cocoa. I'm beginning to understand that you have a thing for chocolate."

"No, I mean *thank you*," I reach over and place a hand on his arm to show I'm not kidding around right now, "for saving me. I don't know what I would have done if you hadn't come by when you did. And, letting everyone know I was okay, bringing me here, giving me shelter, taking care of me...It means a lot."

He seems taken aback by my gratitude and makes a face. "I just did what anyone would have done in the situation. You don't have to thank me."

I shake my head at his naiveté. "On the contrary, in my experience, general kindness and willingness to get involved in someone else's shit is fucking rare."

He shrugs, and his long bangs fall into his green eyes. He's quick to push them back in a well-practiced move. The tattoos on his bare forearms dance in the firelight. "Well, I'm sorry that's been your experience thus far."

"I mean, sure, there are nice people in the world, but most of them don't work in this industry."

He eyes me thoughtfully for too long, and I have to look away. It's too intense. "You're awfully jaded, aren't you?"

I don't even have to think before answering. "I definitely am."

"Then why do you do it? Why stay in a business that you view so negatively?"

Tilting my head to the side as I think, I start to twirl one of my long braids; one of a few habits I've had forever when I think hard about anything. "Just because others are assholes, doesn't mean I have to be one. It's all ego. I can handle ego."

He turns to face me directly, curling a leg under him and stretching an arm on the top of the couch behind me. "But why would you want to subject yourself to that kind of environment voluntarily? I'm not seeing the attraction for you."

"Well..." I try to think how I can explain *why* I do what I do. I don't usually get this introspective about it. I just do my job. "Because I'm responsible for the livelihoods of a lot of people. And not just the band. There are a lot of people who count on me to keep this train rolling. I can't just walk away from that because some asshole hurts my feelings because he doesn't think a woman can do what I do."

"Do you think you're that important?" he asks, but it's not mean. He's genuinely curious.

And that question hits me right in the heart. Right where I've made my job my entire personality. My entire life. I want to think I'm indispensable, but as he's proving with Chaos Fuel, I'm not.

I open my mouth automatically to confirm that, yes, I'm essential to keeping this whole circus going. I'm the glue, the backbone, the master strategist behind the scenes. They'd be lost without the 'Rock Band Dragoness, Mackenzie Roberts' calling the shots.

But the words turn to ashes on my tongue. Self-importance is now a pet peeve of mine. Do I still really think of myself as some savior they couldn't survive without?

I used to. Not any more.

I swallow hard, chasing the fleeting certainty I'm irreplaceable. Maybe before losing Andy. That day something changed. I recognized that chaos governs all, no matter what safeguards I put into place. One drunken night steals a friend and teaches you that you're just another replaceable cog when it comes down to it.

"I think…" I start slowly, "that I have an organized mind others lack. I thrive handling moving parts." Ian leans in, curiosity piqued by my hesitation. "But indispensable?" I sigh. "Nobody is irreplaceable. Even me."

There's a hard truth in acknowledging my expendability that curdles in my gut. I'm not the star power. Never have been. For once, not sure what else to say, I take refuge in my cooling cocoa, eyes downcast.

"I guess anyone could probably do my job," I say, "Not as well, mind you, but sure, anyone could step in and tick the boxes. But they wouldn't know the ins and outs of the dynamics within the band that have formed over the years. Only I do."

He meets my gaze and holds it for a while as he considers my answer. "You care about them. The band."

"Well, yeah. Of course." I can't help but laugh at the crazy situations with the band that pop into my head. But then I remember losing Andy again, and my laughter dies. He's been on my mind often lately. "We've been through a lot together. Walked through the fire and ended up here. We're family."

"Family, huh?"

"Yeah, we're a sort of found family. And, let me tell you, if babysitting those guys is any indication of how stressful parenting is, no, thank you. I'm good."

"You don't want your own family someday? Kids?" Something clouds his expression for a flash before he blinks it away.

I scrunch my nose at the thought. "No. I don't think I'm made for kids. I love them, don't get me wrong. But I'm definitely *not* mom material. I'm just not built that way."

The thought of children pops into my head on occasion, especially with Chelsie's growing brood, but I just can't picture it. Plus, as I just told Ian, I feel responsible for the lives of a lot of people already. I don't want to add to my stress.

I mean, never say never, but I don't think it's in my

cards. And no man thus far has ever made me give it a second thought.

"What makes you think that?" he asks. And he seems genuinely interested, but I'm not sure what to make of that.

Shrugging, I can't think of anything else to add to what I've already said. "I don't know. It's just how I've always been."

He nods and looks away, and for some reason, I feel like I've disappointed him with my answer.

Odd.

CHAPTER 10

HARD NOT TO HOLD YOU

IAN

A strained silence settles around Mackenzie and me once our weighty conversation dies off. I can't deny my deep disappointment at her opinion on motherhood, considering my own family.

So, why the hell didn't I mention my girls?

Oh, you don't want kids? Well, guess what? I have not just one, but two of them. Cross me as a partner off your list right away then.

Something about her being so emphatic against kids just made me clam the fuck up. Like I'd have to defend my own somehow.

It's bloody irrational.

I clear my throat, casting about for a way to recapture the earlier easiness between us. My gaze lands on the bookcase lining the far wall.

"Well, at least there's plenty to read if we get

bored," I say a little too brightly. I cross the room to peruse the eclectic titles, seeking refuge from the sudden tension.

Most are dime-store paperback thrillers and mystery novels, along with some hefty historical biographies. But one slim gold volume stands out, more ornate. *'If...'* is etched in red script across its leather spine. Curious, I crack it open.

My eyes widen as I scan the pages filled with questions. Daring, suggestive questions for lovers like, *'If you could be amazing at only one thing in bed, what would it be?'* Heat floods my cheeks. I snap the book shut, glancing sheepishly back at Mackenzie.

"Find something good?" she asks with a glint in her eye.

"Oh, um...just a book of rather personal questions..." I trail off, hands fidgeting with the binding.

Her eyes sparkle impishly as she holds a hand out for the book. "Let me see. We could trade off and ask each other some."

"What, really?" I blink, taken aback even as curiosity stirs.

"For fun. To get to know each other better." A playful smile tugs her lips. "I'll go first."

"But these questions...I don't know..."

"Come on. What else is there to do?"

Heart quickening, I reluctantly pass her the book. *What have I gotten myself into now?*

A thrill of anticipation chases my nerves as I settle onto the couch next to her.

"Alright then, first question," she begins, mischief dancing in her eyes. The awkwardness between us melts, but the room now crackles with a new tension. She flips through the pages, eyes widening as she reads. "Oh wow. These are...interesting."

"I did tell you they were personal questions," I say, reaching to take the book back from her, but she pulls it out of my reach with a laugh.

"No, no. This could be fun," she says with a sly smile. "Okay, no reading ahead of time. I'll just turn to a page, and where my finger lands is your question, cool?"

My throat goes dry just at the thought of talking about these things with Mackenzie, but she seems interested. At least it will distract from the conversation about kids.

I nod. "Just remember this was your idea."

"Okay, here we go." She licks her lips as she flips pages without looking and points to a spot on a random page. Her cheeks redden, and I instantly regret this. "If you could have changed one thing about the first time you had sex, what would it be?"

She shuts the book loudly and rests her chin on her fist, giving me an intense stare. Her lips are twitching like she's about to break out into raucous laughter.

"Fucking hell," I sigh, rubbing at the scruff on my jaw. "What I'd change about the first time I had sex...Would have been nice to last longer than thirty seconds, for starters."

The bark of laughter Mackenzie lets loose echoes in the cabin, and it's contagious.

"What? It's true," I chuckle, embarrassed. "That poor girl. I had no clue what I was doing."

"Oh no, how old were you?" she asks between giggles.

"God, I was what? Sixteen?" I shake my head. "It was a girl from my neighborhood. Darlene. She was eighteen, and her family was moving away to Inverness. I think it was more out of pity than anything else. Of course, at that age, I didn't care about the why. I just wanted my card punched, you know?"

She pouts, but it's good-natured ribbing. "You poor thing."

"I know. It was very traumatic for all involved." I think the coy smirk now on my face is going to be permanent if I hold it much longer. I grab the book from Mackenzie's lap before she can ask me any more about that embarrassment. "Your turn. Let's see...Hmm." I have to clear my throat as I glance at the question. *This was her idea.* "If you were to name a favorite spot on your body where you liked to be touched, what would it be?"

I steal a look her way as she hears the question, and see her expression roll through about ten emotions. Her cheeks heat, and I have to restrain myself from reaching out to see just how warm she is.

"Yikes. Whose idea was this stupid game?" she laughs nervously.

"I believe it was yours," I say, knowing exactly how smug I look right now.

"Okay, okay, let me think."

"Oh, do take your time."

"Stop it."

"I'm not doing anything."

"Yes, you are. And you know it." She still can't meet my eyes, and it's delicious.

"Fine. I won't say another word." I move as if zipping my lips shut and throwing away a key, but I don't stop watching her squirm. I don't think I've ever seen Mackenzie unsettled like this before, and it's intriguing. Something about knowing she has a delicate side is so fucking attractive. Underneath that hard shell is a softness I didn't know she possessed.

I want to see more of it.

She straightens her shoulders as if steeling herself against her own answer. It's completely quirky, and perfectly Mackenzie. "Well, other than the obvious," her eyes lower, but don't focus on anything in particular, but I get the gist. "I would say my neck."

Her fingers seem to automatically go to the spot, and my willpower disappears. I reach out and graze my fingertips slowly along the skin just below her ear, reveling in the softness of it.

"Here?" I ask. My voice is rougher than normal as my throat tightens.

Goosebumps rise on her skin, and she shivers as she closes her eyes at my touch. A small gasp escapes her lips, and I'm instantly hard. Knowing that one simple touch from me can get someone like Mackenzie aroused is more than a turn-on. It's the stuff wet dreams are made of. And not just *'someone like'* Mackenzie, but *actually* Mackenzie. It boggles my mind.

Her sharp intake of breath emboldens me. I trace light circles, documenting her reactions. Each new swirl pulls a whispered gasp from her lips. I'm drunk on this power, on the headiness of reducing steely Mackenzie Roberts to putty with a mere caress.

My fingers linger, and she doesn't move away. I don't want to stop touching her, but as I see her braced leg out of the corner of my eye, I know this is an unusual situation. She might still be under the effects of morphine, and not clear in her thoughts. I don't want to do something she'll regret in the brighter light of day.

Part of me warns that I'm taking advantage, that this intimacy is only born of extenuating circumstances and medication. But another darker part whirls in exhilaration at this first crack in her armor, this glimpse beneath the surface at the warm, wanting woman within.

Reluctantly, I pull my hand back. "Sorry," I whisper. "I couldn't help myself when you pointed out the spot." I don't really have a good excuse for why I touched her other than I couldn't stop myself, and that's not an excuse at all.

Her eyes open slowly, and she seems to come out of a trance as she focuses on the fire. "No, it's fine. Really." She won't look my way, and I don't know what to make of that. Maybe I did go too far. "I should probably get some sleep. I'm having a hard time keeping my eyes open."

I study her for a second, looking for a lie, but not seeing one. Of course, she's probably exhausted. I need to get my mind out of the fucking gutter, and back into reality.

Getting up from the couch, I jump into action. "Right. Wait here. I'll get everything ready for you."

"But--"

I don't let her finish her protest, and hurry to the bedroom to prepare the room for her. Knowing she doesn't have any of her luggage with her, I lay out one of my T-shirts and a pair of sweatpants with a drawstring waist. In the én suite bathroom, I double-check that there are toiletries she can use and a toothbrush.

When I emerge, I'm surprised to find Mackenzie in the middle of the room on her crutches, a scowl on her face.

"Are you okay?" I ask, rushing over to her to assist if she needs it.

She waves me off, clearly exhausted. "Yeah, yeah.

I'm fine. I just hate being an imposition. You rented this nice cabin, and here I am taking your bed. It doesn't seem fair."

I force my mind to skip over the short list of risqué retorts it was instantly planning to let loose and stumble into modesty.

"Don't even think twice about it," I say, helping to usher her into the room. "As I said, I'm glad I can be of assistance." I watch her carefully as she moves around, making sure she seems steady. "Do you want me to stick around or help you with anything?"

I shove my hands in my pockets, trying not to appear as awkward as I'm feeling at the moment.

She surveys the room quickly and shakes her head confidently, finally meeting my eyes. "I'll be okay. Thank you again for everything, Ian."

The sound of my name in her voice stirs something in me that I haven't tapped into in a very long time, and I can only nod. I don't entirely trust my voice.

Finally, after an extended beat, I back out of the doorway. "Goodnight, Mackenzie."

"Goodnight."

What an interesting evening.

I'm speeding down the slope again, icy wind biting my cheeks. My skis slice through glittering powder, legs burning as I push my limits. I feel powerful, invincible.

Until the ground disappears beneath me.

My stomach lurches as I sail off the cliff's edge, suspended hauntingly in the air. Desperately I twitch in my sleep, trying to turn my phantom skis back to solid ground.

But gravity takes over. The earth rushes up in a blur of white and red. I start to slide and can't stop. I'm going to slide off the earth. Blinding pain splinters through my leg as it smashes against unforgiving metal.

I jolt awake with a scream trapped in my throat; sheets tangled around me. Cold sweat chills my skin. Within the dark cocoon of blankets, I can't stifle a sob, tears spilling down my cheeks.

"Just a nightmare," I repeat it like a mantra, clutching my throbbing leg. But the dark room echoing my ragged breaths is strange. I don't know this room. I feel so lost, wounded, alone.

My heart threatens to pound out of my chest. I've never felt so shaken, so unable to pull myself back together.

The door to the bedroom flies open, and light from the hallway pours in. I squint as Ian's silhouette rushes toward me.

"Mackenzie, what is it? What's wrong?" The worry in his voice only seems to intensify everything wrong with me.

My mind replays the accident over and over, and my leg is as painful as it was when it happened.

"I just...I don't know," I say, and it comes out as a squeak. "It was a bad dream."

He's at my side in an instant, arms wrapping around me and pulling me to him. I don't fight him, and allow myself to feel safe as I bury my face into his chest. I can't seem to catch my breath.

"I've got you. It was just a nightmare. Hush," he soothes, rocking me and smoothing my hair. "It's alright. You're safe now. You're safe here."

As I wake up more, the pain in my leg seems to lessen, and the embarrassment of the situation starts to dawn on me. I'm acting like a child; crying over a bad dream. This is really above and beyond dramatic. Ian's going to think I'm a fool.

That's when I notice that he's not wearing a shirt, and I've been blubbering into his bare chest. His well-toned bare chest. That smells amazing.

Shit.

I pull away abruptly and wipe unceremoniously at my watery eyes, sniffling. "Sorry. I didn't mean to wake you. I'm fine now. Thanks. Sorry."

He's still holding my shoulders, but now at arm's length. I can feel him studying me in the golden sliver of light from the hall and I want nothing more than to crawl under this bed and hide. I feel like a complete idiot.

"It's quite alright." He hesitates, and I can feel his body tense slightly as he tries to piece together what to do with a hysterical woman in his bed. "Are you sure you're okay? What about your leg? You were holding it when I first came in. Is it hurting?"

He actually sounds like he doesn't think I'm crazy or being overly dramatic. He's genuinely concerned. It surprises me, but also makes me consider his question.

It only takes a split second to realize that, yes, my leg is really hurting. I nod. "Yeah. I must have moved around too much in my sleep."

"Or, the pain could be why you had the nightmare in the first place."

"Chicken. Egg. Either way, it's scrambled," I say, not caring which came first, or what caused what. I just hurt.

"Right. Let me get one of your pain pills," he says, and before I can protest, he's gone and back with a pain pill and a glass of water.

I take both from him, my hands only shaking slightly. I still feel like a little kid for some reason, needing to be tended to like this. Staring at the pill for a second, I debate not taking it, but the pain wins out, and I down it before I can think too hard about it.

"Can I ask you a personal question?" He asks, cautious.

"More personal than the ones from earlier?" I can feel myself blush, and move to set the water on the bedside table to hide my face in the low light.

He lifts a shoulder in a half-shrug. "It's not a sexual question."

I don't know if I should be relieved or disappointed. "Okay..."

"Why were you so against the pain medicine earlier?" His voice isn't accusing, or judgmental. Just curious.

The question surprises me for some reason. I guess I didn't think he was paying that close of attention to any of that in the hospital. Apparently, he notices everything. And retains it. Good to know.

It takes me a minute to gather myself and find a way to express what my thought process was.

I let out a long breath, reposition the pillows under my leg, and lean back against the headboard. "When Andy died, I had a good friend who had a hard time dealing with it. They had a problem with narcotics for a little while after that. It became a crutch and a way to not deal with anything." I swallow hard, pushing myself to talk but still keep it vague. "The friend I knew disappeared for a while, drowned by grief and narcotics. They scared us...scared me. It killed me to just look on powerlessly as they sank further down that hole. It was hard to watch, and I don't want to go through that or put anyone else through it."

"Jake?" he asks, again not judging.

I don't want to name Jake. It's his business, and I'm not about to expose him. But I don't want to lie to Ian either, so I say nothing. Jake's downward spiral after the accident, and then his thinking he caused it was one of the worst things I've witnessed. If there's even a sliver of a chance that spiral could happen to me, I want no part of it.

Ian nods quietly, understanding. "I see." He shifts his weight, making the bed rock a little. "Well, I can watch over you with that, if you'd like. You know, I can hold them for you, and you'll have to go through me to get them if you're that worried about it. A safeguard."

Still no judgment from him. On any of this. I get the feeling it takes a lot to ruffle Ian Summer's feathers. His face is in shadow with the light from the hall behind him, but I can imagine the kindness on his face, his green eyes gentle and intense at the same time.

"You'd do that for me?" I ask. I'm not used to

people offering to help me, and I'm really not accustomed to actually letting them. I'm the problem solver, not the problem.

"Of course." He takes my hand into his, and it's exactly what I need at this moment. He seems to know exactly what to say, and what to do to put me at ease.

"Thank you." I barely get the words out before a gigantic yawn overtakes me. I know it's not the pain pill yet. I'm just exhausted. But, I also don't want to fall right back into that nightmare again either.

"Well, I should let you get some sleep," he says, moving to get up from the bed. I grip his hand tighter and hold him in place. I don't want to be alone right now. Not yet.

"Don't," I say, not sure what exactly I'm doing. "Can you stay with me? Just until I fall asleep?" My voice is so timid I don't recognize it. All of this is so out of character for me. I'm not a damsel in distress. But I am being honest with myself. I don't want to be left here in this strange bed and room by myself. It's irrational, but it is what it is.

He hesitates. Probably considering if I have other intentions besides just falling asleep. I hadn't thought of that. It wasn't a proposition.

I'm about to tell him as much when he gets up and goes out to the hall to turn out the light. For a second, I think he's just going to leave, but then he rounds the bed and sits next to me on top of the covers.

"Come here," he says, holding his arms open for

me, and I don't argue. The recent safety I felt in his arms when I woke up was enough for me to crave it again.

I carefully readjust myself, so my leg is still elevated but nestle into the crook of his arm. He gives me a small squeeze as he stretches his legs and crosses his ankles.

"Shall I tell you a bedtime story as well?" he asks, resting his chin on the top of my head.

"You'd better," I smile. I could get used to this.

"Hmm. Once upon a time, there was this super smart rock 'n roll band manager who thought she knew how to ski..."

"She sounds amazing."

"She is. She can do many things. But she can't ski for shit." His chest rumbles as he chuckles.

I don't know how the rest of the story goes, or if I even hear it. I fall fast asleep before I can learn any more about the amazing skiing band manager.

CHAPTER 12

HEAD OVER HEELS

IAN

The wind howling and the sound of ice hitting the windows wake me. As awareness trickles in, yesterday comes rushing back - the accident, the storm, Mackenzie shaking with sobs in the darkness.

She's still curled against me, her head tucked under my chin, breaths deep and even. Something in my chest clenches realizing she trusted me enough to fall asleep in my arms. I don't dare move yet, unwilling to disturb this peace.

Her braids are undone, and her hair spills over the pillow in a riot of purple jewel tones. I trail a tentative hand down the strands, suddenly appreciating the vulnerability of her like this. Her usual kinetic energy is muted. Her features are smooth and untroubled for a change.

I let myself imagine, just for a moment, waking up beside her becoming routine, comforted by each other's presence. My fingers trail feather-light patterns on her shoulder. What would it be like to wake up with her every day? To have someone steadily in my life again?

The thought brings up equal parts longing and doubt within me. My divorce was three years ago, and I've had fleeting relationships since, but none of them even ignited a flicker of this kind of thinking.

What makes Mackenzie so different? Her intellect, for one thing. If she doesn't know something, she makes it her business to find it out. And her intuition is unmatched. She can read a person or situation like a book. These qualities lend themselves nicely to her work ethic. Which is beyond principled. It's personal to her, and I love that. All of that put together is enough to get me on board.

With a silent sigh, I carefully extricate myself from Mackenzie's side, tucking the blankets around her. I stand still for a moment, taking in this vision to carry with me before turning to face reality again and whatever Mother Nature has in store for us today. From the chill I'm already feeling, it's not good.

As I gaze out the large front window of the cabin to gauge the storm, I can barely see twenty feet from where I stand, the falling snow is so thick. It's then that I notice how quiet it is in the cabin.

Eerily quiet.

I know that snow dampens sound, but that's outside. Inside, there's usually at least some sort of white noise, but there's just nothing. My stomach clenches as possibilities dawn on me. The most likely culprit -

No power.

I hurry to the kitchen area and flip the wall switch.

Nothing.

Fuck.

Frowning, I confirm none of the light switches work in the silent cabin. Of course, the bloody blizzard knocked out the power. I debate rousing Mackenzie to tell her, but she looked so peaceful. I'll let her rest while I handle this.

I need to take action now.

First, I quietly pile logs in the stone fireplace, getting a healthy blaze going to combat the chill in the air. At least we won't freeze. Surveying the wall of frosted glass, I see the snow still whipping past relentlessly. We could be stuck here awhile.

Rustling through the pantry, I take inventory - bottled water, flashlights, and ample nonperishables. Between the fire and bounty of blankets I brought to Mackenzie's room, we have the essentials covered. While taking out items for breakfast, I make a mental note not to open the refrigerator or freezer anymore unless absolutely necessary. I suppose some food items could be stored outside if it comes to it.

I scrub a hand down my face, calculating. There's

not much left now, but to make her comfortable and find ways to pass the time until help...or at least electricity returns. I stare into the whiteout, schemes turning despite a tickle of anticipation at the extra privacy. This situation is unexpected, but in all honesty, not entirely unwelcome since I get to spend it with Mackenzie.

Luckily, the stove is gas, and I'm able to use it to cook and boil water for coffee. I find a French press in one of the cabinets, and after some trial and error, manage to get some decent coffee out of it.

With basic necessities stable for us for now and breakfast on tap, my thoughts turn to wider unknowns. I dig my phone from where my ski pants were abandoned on the bedroom floor. No signal bars show on the phone screen, unsurprisingly, but I open recent contacts to message status updates while I can. Maybe they can go through if the reception is intermittent. My phone battery is only at a miserable fifteen percent. I should have charged it overnight, but I had no clue the power would go out.

Fingers hovering over the band chat, I debate worrying anyone when we're helpless to do anything until conditions improve. I guess it's better to quell any assumptions that we're somehow ignoring problems, though.

> ME: Power out @ cabin. Snowed in but safe Any issues there?

Knowing everyone is probably still sleeping, I press enter, imagining the chaotic possibilities of so many bands unsupervised during a storm and a blackout, and wince. But any mess can wait. Keeping the musicians calm overrides anything else for now.

The message appears to go through when there's a blip of reception, so I tap another number and press my ear to the phone as it struggles to connect the call. "Hey Tony," I rush in my old executive tone when the hotel manager picks up. All business. "This is Ian Summer with Blackmore Records. I'm snowed in with no power at the moment. How's it looking there?" I brace myself, only relaxing when reassurances come that, despite the current situation, and outside of some expected rowdiness in the hotel bar, things are reasonably under control, and by all reports from the production crew, the festival is still on.

The call isn't long, as it drops almost as soon as it starts. My mind is at ease, though. Mackenzie's will be too.

Bacon pops and sizzles in the pan when shuffling behind me alerts me that Mackenzie's awake. I glance over as she emerges wrapped in a blanket, expertly maneuvering herself around furniture on crutches. My shirt and sweats from yesterday dwarf her frame.

"Power's out from the storm," I say, shutting the stove burners off to give her my full attention. "But I stoked up the fireplace and took stock of supplies, so we're all set for—"

"My hero," she interrupts, playfully batting her eyes as she makes a beeline for the fancy coffee machine, nonplussed to find it inactive. Amused, I watch her rummage through cabinets undeterred. "Should I propose again?"

"If the whim takes you,"

"Impressive work, though, in crisis management," she tosses over her shoulder. "Making fire, preparing sustenance. Very 'rugged mountain man' of you. Do you chop wood too? Women on TikTok go crazy for that sort of thing."

I snort. "Just basic Boy Scout stuff. Though if you keep up that flattery, I may have to demonstrate my Wolf Cub survival skills further."

Her eyebrow quirks up. "Careful, or I'll hold you to that." A grin flashes, and my chest warms despite the room's lingering chill.

Before I can get flustered, I insist she relax while I finish preparing breakfast. "You. Sit. I'll take care of everything," I say, ushering her to a stool at the island.

"But--"

"But nothing. Consider yourself off duty today."

She sits, but pouts, and it's fucking adorable. Noticing her phone on the counter next to mine, she reaches for it, and the pout deepens.

"It's dead, Jim," she mutters, mournfully pushing the inert technology away.

I arch an eyebrow. "Are you a Trekkie?"

"Hmm?" she asks, distracted. "Oh, no. Well, maybe. I guess. Yeah."

"So definitive."

"Sorry, I'm still waking up." She winces slightly as she shifts her weight.

"Well, I hope you got some rest after your...Shall I dispense some pain relief now to head off the worst?" I decide not to bring up her nightmare, or my resulting night spent next to her in bed. I've had enough stray thoughts about it all morning, and need to keep myself in check.

She considers my question and nods. "That's probably a good idea."

Before she can second guess herself, I head back into the bedroom where I've hidden the bottle of pills in my duffle bag and give it to her. She's definitely going to need it, and it's better to get ahead of the pain than try to catch up to it.

She takes it without complaint and accepts the plate of food and cup of coffee I put in front of her. Taking a delicate bite out of a piece of bacon, she eyes me curiously. "So, about last night..."

Oh boy, here we go.

"So, about last night..."

He doesn't respond, so I stir my coffee, grasping for the right words. Last night was crazy. The vivid nightmare, my pathetic weeping spell, Ian's tender reassurances, falling asleep cradled against his chest. Heat prickles my cheeks, remembering. That doesn't even include our 'getting to know you' personal questions.

God, where do I even begin?

I risk a glance up at him through my lashes. He's attempting to appear nonchalant, focusing intently on scrubbing some non-existent speck off the counter, but tension pulls at the corded muscle in his forearm. At least I'm not the only awkward one.

"Thank you, by the way," I offer softly. "For coming

in when I was upset. And staying. You didn't have to do that."

Ian tosses the dishrag aside, leaning against the counter to finally meet my eyes. His expression is unreadable. "Of course, I did. I wasn't about to leave you frightened and in pain."

His gaze gentles, stirring that now familiar warmth in my core. "I meant what I said about being here for you. However you need. Just say the word."

My lungs constrict oddly in my chest. I press on before dwelling on the meaning behind my breathlessness. "Thank you, I appreciate that. Last night was...well, a lot." I give a self-deprecating laugh, willing a lighter mood to manifest. I don't want things to get too heavy between us again. Not this early, anyway.

"Don't mention it." He turns away, and I'm not sure if he just gets embarrassed with gratitude directed at him, or what, but it's endearing nonetheless.

I clear my throat, hoping a shift back to professional topics might settle us both. "So...I realize with everything going on, I never checked on how things are with everyone else at the hotel. Any word?"

Ian latches onto the subject change with visible relief. "Oh, right. Well, I touched base with hotel management this morning, at least. The power is out there, too. But apparently, everything is fairly under control. And the local production manager says the festival is still a go apparently, despite the weather."

"No wild parties raging in our absence, then? That's a surprise." I try for wry humor.

His lips quirk. "Fortunately nothing major. Just some expected hotel bar rowdiness. The bands seem to be faring alright together despite the close quarters. No clashing of egos. Yet. Though, I'm sure they wish their fearless leaders were on site."

"Fearless leaders, I like the sound of that." I sip my cooling coffee, puzzled to feel a pang of guilt that chaotic forces beyond my control have me waylaid here instead. I'm not feeling very leader-ish at the moment. Ian said things were fine, but still...

"I'm sure your crew has everything running smoothly even if we're holed up here," Ian offers gently, reading the turn of my thoughts easily now. "Try not to worry unless word comes otherwise."

He pauses, picks up his phone, and briefly reads something. Frowning, he nervously avoids my gaze. But suddenly he looks bemused.

I brace myself. "What? Do you know something I don't?"

"Well...fuck," Ian rubs his jaw. "I guess the hotel manager didn't tell me everything. I may have just learned of some emerging chaos."

I raise an eyebrow. "Oh? Do tell."

"Don't panic. It's not about your flock. It's a

message from the festival director about my guys in Chaos Fuel."

He rotates his phone screen to me, showing a brief text chain. My eyes widen, taking in vague reports of alcohol-fueled disputes early this morning between band members now threatening to derail their spot in the upcoming concert.

Figures.

"Shit," I breathe out. "Didn't you just have some personnel changes too? Is the new guy not meshing?"

Ian visibly winces. "That's part of it." He scrolls some more, "Our rookie bassist is apparently rubbing certain bandmates the wrong way. And our drummer has discovered the minibar... They are their band name personified. Bloody chuckleheads."

I press two fingers to my temple as scenarios play out in my mind. At least with my guys happily domesticated, the drama lies solely with Ian's motley crew. Though, it's making me feel bad for him.

"Is there anything you need to do?" I can tell he's not happy with the situation. I don't blame him.

He tosses his phone back onto the counter, defeated. I hate to see it. "There's nothing I *can* do even if I wanted to. Just lost service again." Raising his arms to rub the back of his neck, his t-shirt lifts, exposing a mighty fine set of abs I didn't know he was hiding.

My body seems to react of its own volition at the sight of his bare skin, and I have to shift in my seat.

The pain meds may be dulling the pain in my leg, but they are certainly not muting everything my body feels.

I know the responsible thing would be for him to convene an emergency band meeting of some kind, and stop the mayhem in its tracks. If he could even get cell service. But the glow in Ian's eyes kicks up long-dormant mischievousness in me.

Besides, we're cut off from that right now. A distraction for both of us might be exactly what we both need. Wouldn't it be bliss to pretend just a bit longer that we're the only people in the world?

After years of being hyper-focused on my career, and the accident yesterday, I think I'm due an indulgence for once. And isolating here with Ian already feels like stolen magic outside of real life's demands.

Fuck it.

"Well, it looks like we're stranded here for a while. So how about we play hooky from management duty to focus on more..." I trail a suggestive glance down his toned body, feeling bold, "...pressing matters?"

I relish his sudden flush. Outside chaos be damned, I'm rather enjoying this forced hibernation with my handsome English rescuer.

His flush turns into a smolder as the ember ignites in him, too, and he leans over the counter, coming face to face with me. Those emerald eyes of his are intense. "It sounds as if you have something in mind. Dare I ask what it might be?"

I mirror him and lean forward, a breath away from a kiss. Glancing between his lips and his eyes enticingly, I scrape a fingernail lightly along the stubble on his jawline. "Oh, I don't know...I thought maybe we could pick up where we left off on our literary adventure from last night." A devilish smile plays on my lips as I watch his pupils dilate, knowing that I'm getting to him as much as he is getting to me. "If you're up for it, that is."

He returns the favor and rubs the pad of his thumb gently across my bottom lip, sending shivers straight down my spine. "Oh, I'm up for it," he says, his voice smooth.

I reluctantly pull away from his touch, missing it the instant we part.

This is going to be fun.

"Then, let the games begin."

CHAPTER 14

LIKE REAL PEOPLE DO

IAN

My pulse thrums as Mackenzie fixes me with a heated gaze, lower lip caught alluringly between her teeth. "Let the games begin," she says, voice dropping an octave.

I track her slow progress crossing the room, injury forcing an enticing sway to her hips. She glances back coyly as she settles onto the couch. "You coming?"

Wetting my lips, I choke down a raunchy reply, trailing after her in a daze. Is this actually happening? After our continuous charged but restrained attraction, rational thought melts away as I imagine where this might lead.

I always did have an overactive imagination.

"So..." I begin croakily once I join her, grasping for some shred of eloquence but failing miserably. "You, uh...mentioned a game?" *Smooth, Romeo,* I scold myself even as Mackenzie's mouth curves into a smile that short-circuits my brain even further.

She leans in conspiratorially, bracing a hand on my knee. "I thought we could revisit a certain book you introduced me to last night." Her gaze flickers salaciously down my torso again. She needs to stop doing that, or this could accelerate quickly. "If you think you can handle where that might lead."

I swallow hard, all remaining blood flow redirected decidedly southward. Handle it? At this rate, I may bloody well combust. But if this exquisite torture is my fate, so be it.

"Shall I go first?" I ask, sliding the book off the coffee table, and flipping the pages while holding her gaze. Her eager anticipation is infectious, and my dick twitches in response. "Right. Here we are. If you had to name the smallest space you've ever had sex in, what would it be?"

I glance up, determined to no longer be embarrassed by these questions. We're both adults here. These are normal topics of conversation between consenting adults. Sort of.

My internal assumption that it would be a tour bus bathroom is quickly dismissed when she says, "There's a green room closet at The Wheelhouse in London that is barely two feet by two feet. It's not even big enough to store a mop and a bucket. But some creative positioning..."

I've been to shows there, both my own and while

scouting, but don't recall ever seeing this closet she's talking about. "Indeed. Creativity can come in handy sometimes." My mind starts reeling again with imagined sexual scenarios with Mackenzie, here in the cabin. Positions...

She interrupts my thoughts by stealing the book from my grasp, shutting it, and opening it quickly, letting the pages spread naturally. Pointing to a random spot on the page, her fingers tremble slightly as she reads the question aloud. "If you had to name the one person who most truly tested your sexual self-restraint, who would it be?"

Glancing up at me, her violet eyes flash with interest, and maybe I'm imagining this too, but I think I see hope. She has to know my answer. She has to know that it's her. Right this very minute.

Slowly, I take the book from her and place it on the table. She doesn't resist, and this encourages me more.

Leaning close, I reach up to touch her neck, precisely sliding my fingers from the point just below her ear that I know she likes and around to gently pull her closer. "How about I show you?" I say, brushing my lips against hers. I pull back to check her reaction, and her eyes remain closed, lips parted. My cock strains against the restriction of my boxers, putting my aforementioned self-restraint to the test.

Surprisingly, Mackenzie slides her hands up my chest to my shoulders and pulls me down into a deep, soul-searching kiss, sending my pulse into overdrive.

Our tongues are in sync, and it's not like the usual 'we've never kissed before' awkward discovery of the other person. We kiss like we've done it a thousand times before, and it's what we live for.

What we would die for.

A moan, deep in her throat, spurs me on, and I slide my hand under her t-shirt, grazing the soft skin of her torso with my fingers. Goosebumps rise in my wake as I cup her breast, her nipple erect and sensitive to my touch. A slight squeeze and her body arches, forcing our kiss to end as she inhales sharply.

Her hands grope under my own shirt, nails dragging along my back as I kiss a hot trail down her throat, stretching the neck of the shirt to get to her collarbone. Another small twist of her hard nipple, and one of her hands immediately and deftly finds my cock through my sweatpants, her fingers tracing the outline and finding the end of it protruding from the waistband of my boxers. When fully erect, I cannot be contained by mere underwear. The only thing between her hand and the most sensitive part of my cock is a thin layer of jersey.

She inhales a breath at what I hope is a pleasant surprise at her discovery. Gently, I lean her back on the couch lengthwise, being extremely careful of her brace, and lift her shirt up to expose her beautiful breasts. The cool air of the room stiffens her nipples even more, and I have to taste them. Pressing one between my fingers, I devour the other with my mouth, tongue swirling teasingly as I suck. I lavish the sensitive peak, utterly lost now in sweet torment. Her back arches, and she grinds her pelvis against my hip, seeking friction.

I know that desire because I feel it too. I want to be inside of her more than I want to breathe at this moment. I need to worship every devastating inch of her until we're both drunk on pleasure. I'm drowning in our sexual tension and only crave release. A release only she can give.

I release the other nipple, and my fingers skim lower of their own volition to her inner thigh, feeling her stomach clench beneath me as I caress her slowly. She pushes against my hand as she kisses my shoulder, grazing her teeth along the fabric of my shirt.

We need to lose these clothes.

A sharp knocking on the cabin door freezes us both in place. We're breathing hard and glance at each other in confusion.

"Did you hear that?" I ask. Maybe I imagined it.

Before she can answer, another knock echoes through the room.

Fuck. Who could be out in this weather?

"Hold that thought," I say, leaning in to steal a kiss before pushing myself off the couch and rearranging my bits and pieces so I can walk somewhat properly to answer the door.

I glance over my shoulder to ensure that Mackenzie is decent before opening the door to see who it is. Cold wind and snow charge into the cabin as I discover Billy on the doorstep. His beard has icicles dangling from it, and his nose is almost as red as the hat on his head.

"Billy, come in out of the weather," I say, stepping aside. The cold air at least assists in deflating my sex drive, as it were.

He accepts my invitation gladly and stomps his feet on the carpet runner near the door, clapping and rubbing his hands together, shedding snow and ice all over the floor.

"Thanks, Ian," he nods to me, then to Mackenzie, "Ma'am. I just wanted to check on you folks since you're not from around here. I figured you might need a hand with the power going out and all, but I see from the nice fire you got going you two are doin' alright."

"Yes, we're keeping quite warm," I say, a glint in my eye as I nod at Mackenzie. She doesn't even blush, just smiles quietly over the back of the couch at us.

"I've been telling the Lancaster's to get a generator for this sort of thing since it happens so often, but they're big city types that don't understand the weather up here."

"I see." I get the feeling that if I let him, Billy will talk our ears off, and that is the absolute last thing I currently want to happen. But, I'm nothing if not polite. "Can I get you a coffee or something else warm to drink? You look a bit like a snowman."

He waves me off jovially. "Oh no, I need to get back

out there. I'm helping out with the plowing of the main roads as much as I can. Can't beat the old snowcat for getting around the snow and ice." He holds a gloved hand out for me to shake. "Anyway, glad to see you two are doing okay. Don't forget to call if you need anything."

"Will do," I say, shutting the door behind him as he leaves, the howling wind resigned to the outdoors once again.

I lean back against the wood frame, taking in the sight of Mackenzie smiling at me from the couch. Her lips are a bit swollen from our kisses, and her cheeks are still flushed from exertion. The muss of her long hair only accentuates her sexiness. She bites her bottom lip suggestively, and my dick responds right away like we were never interrupted.

"So, where were we?" I ask, heading back to the couch.

"So, where were we?" Ian asks, coming back to me on the couch. Like either of us could really forget. He leans over the back and brushes his lips against mine so softly it's more breath than contact, and it gives me shivers. "Right about there, if I'm not mistaken."

I smile against him briefly but lean back, my mind finally catching up with my body. Yes, I've always thought Ian was attractive, and even more so now that I've gotten to know him better, but this is a dangerous line we're about to cross.

It wouldn't be the first time I've hooked up with someone from the industry. It's fairly commonplace, considering the nature of our jobs and the close proximity we have to each other at times. Especially on the road. Sometimes, you take what you can get when you're in the mood.

Not that I bed or bus hop. Quite the opposite. If asked, most would tell you I'm a prude since I suck so much at flirting and turn most people down. But I'm not. I'm just extremely selective. And discreet.

But this feels different.

Am I feeling this way because we're basically trapped together right now? Am I just killing time in a very pleasant and sexy way? Is it because he rescued me yesterday? I feel like I owe him somehow? I don't think I would do that. Or is it the pain meds? Am I not in my right mind?

I evaluate myself quickly and feel as though I am in control of my faculties. So, it's not that. At least I don't think it is. How would I know?

Could it be that I'm catching feelings for Ian? I don't usually do feelings. It's too complicated and messy. One, I don't have time for it. And, two, I don't fucking have time for it. My job is my life. I don't have the energy or the inclination to be responsible for someone else's feelings at the moment. I don't want to console someone who doesn't understand me and how I tick.

"Hey, you okay?" he asks, searching my eyes.

I swallow hard, not understanding why this situation has me so mixed up. It should be pretty cut and dry. I don't know why this feels like new territory for me. "We probably need to talk about this."

He arches a brow but rounds the couch to sit next to me, giving me his full attention. "Okay, what would you like to talk about?"

I stare at him, a little dumbfounded. Does he not see a problem with what we're doing? Of course not. He's a guy. Nothing is ever complicated until you spell it out and give a diagram or list with bullet points, or a fucking PowerPoint presentation. Then they get it. Usually.

Ian isn't stupid, he should get this.

"Do you not think we should talk about what just happened?" I ask, willing him to not be typical. Trying to manifest a real complex human in him.

"Well, of course, but there are several issues," he says, rubbing at his stubbly chin. I must say, he looks good with a partial beard. Definitely brings out more of the 'rugged mountain man' vibe. "I just wondered which one you wanted to discuss."

I tilt my head, confused. "Several?"

"Well, yeah. One - Do we or don't we have sex? I will need your explicit consent, obviously. Two - If we do have sex, what does that mean for us personally and professionally? And three - What position do you prefer? I don't think we got to that part of the book yet, and inquiring minds want to know." He grins, and it's cheeky as hell.

I love it.

Any fear I may have had that Ian was, deep down, a typical misogynistic jerk is quickly set aside. I should have known better than to doubt him. But then, don't I doubt everyone? Maybe I shouldn't.

"Well, since you seem to be so on top of everything, why don't you pick one of those?" I know as soon as I say it that I shouldn't have. He's going to go straight to the position question.

Surprisingly, while he did have that look about him that he wanted to go that route, he doesn't. But, he's still siding on humor.

"Here's the thing," he starts. "As for the 'do we or don't we' portion of the menu, I'll pick the 'we do.' The question is, do you agree?"

Something about how he's phrasing everything is messing with my head for some reason. Like he's not taking this seriously enough. But why am I taking it *so* seriously? I've never done this before. Usually, if I'm in the mood, and a reasonable opportunity presents itself, I just do what I need to without a second thought. I'm completely overthinking this.

"I think I do..." I say, biting my lip, suddenly unsure.

His brow furrows. "So, what's changed in the last few minutes? Because I was under the impression, and tell me if I'm way off base here, that you were into it as much as I was. Am. You know what I mean."

Now he's flustered. Great. I'm screwing this all up. Maybe I'm not thinking straight after all. Maybe the pain meds are messing with my thought process. That can't be a good thing when it comes to something like this.

I meet his eyes, and behind the passion that I see there, I see concern. I wasn't expecting that.

"Honestly, I don't know if the pain meds are clouding my judgment or not."

He puts a hand on my thigh and squeezes lightly. The warmth of his hand is comforting. "Say no more. Sex is officially off the menu." He smiles, and it's genuine. Not the pouty disappointment that would typically accompany this change in direction. "And you're right. We probably should talk more about it before taking that step...If we ever take it, that is. Not that I don't want to, because, of course, I do...I just. Tell you what, I'll just shut up now. How's that?"

That makes me laugh and breaks the tension that has been slowly building between us since we started talking. I'm glad he's reacting this way.

"Okay, good. Thanks. I mean, I know I kind of started it, but..."

"It doesn't matter if you started it or not. You're stopping it. End of story. Next subject."

I almost propose again, but stop myself. I'm not sure if I'd be joking or not anymore. That just goes to show how muddled my mind is right now. So, I guess it's a good thing we're not going any farther.

"Next subject," I repeat. "What is the next subject?"

He studies me carefully. Intently. "What about the

possibility of it? Someday. Could that be a thing? And if so, what would it mean? Or, do to our relationship? If anything."

"Would we be crossing some sort of professional line, you think?" I ask, curious what he thinks about the idea.

Crossing his arms, he considers. "I don't think so. I'm not your boss, and you're not mine, so that's not a problem. And if I remember correctly, my contract only stipulates not to fuck around with the talent."

"Same."

"Not to say that you're not talented. I'm sure you have many talents."

"Ha ha."

"Do you have any talents?" he asks, a smirk curving his lips.

While I know what he's secretly referring to, I have to think for a minute. It's been a while since I've even had a hobby, let alone a talent.

"I used to be able to twirl a baton," I say, almost proud of it even though it was years ago, and I barely even remember it.

"Oh? Were you in marching band?"

"No. It was just for fun."

"You'd twirl a baton...For fun?" The surprise and doubt in his expression are laughable like it's the weirdest thing he's ever heard.

"Yes. It was something my friend Chelsie and I would do after school. We taught ourselves how to do it." I stick my chin out defiantly. "We thought we were very cool."

His eyebrows lift. "Oh, I'm sure you were extremely cool. No question. Coolest kid on your block."

"Oh, stop it. You're just jealous because I bet you can't twirl a baton. Admit it."

"You win that bet." His smile is relaxed, and I love how easily we fall into conversations like this. It's completely random, but at the same time, so insightful. Not necessarily about my baton twirling as a kid, but things like this give a glimpse of what made us who we are today. Like him being a Boy Scout when he was younger, it made an impression on him that survives to this day. And luckily, saved me.

"What about you?" I ask. "Any talents other than making hot cocoa from scratch and cooking amazing breakfasts?"

"Well..."

"Or building fires? Soothing nightmares? Saving damsels?" I go on, knowing that instead of stroking his ego, it's actually embarrassing him a little. It's not my intention, but he needs to stop being so humble. "Don't you play guitar? Or is it bass?" I feel bad that I don't know this about him. I'm not sure if we've ever talked about it and I just don't remember, or if I never really knew.

"Both, really. But mainly bass, yeah." He again isn't bragging, though he probably should be. "Give me any stick with strings on it, and I can probably play it. Well..." His voice trails off.

"What happened with your band?" I ask, wanting to know so much more about this man who seems to have it all together. There's got to be chinks in his shining armor somewhere. "Why did you guys break up? And why didn't you keep on with music?"

A shadow seems to cross over his features, like a storm front moving in. Maybe I shouldn't have asked about it. Or, maybe he doesn't want to talk about it.

"Now, that is a long story," he says, focusing intently on the fire. I can feel him tense up next to me, his shoulders rising slightly.

"We've got nothing but time," I say quietly, not wanting to push him too far on it. "If you want to tell it. You don't have to."

CHAPTER 16

CONFESSION BOX

IAN

I flex my hand unconsciously, the ghost ache of arthritis flaring that always comes along with bad weather. Mackenzie regards me patiently, with no judgment in her open expression. Rubbing my jaw, I debate baring my long-buried pains to her, but I don't want to put any more barriers between us. She's been open and honest with me. It's only fair that I do the same, about this at least. No matter how painful.

I take the leap.

"So, you know Corpse Limousine imploded. What you may not know is that it was over a girl." I give a doleful laugh. "Isn't it always, somehow?" I run a hand through my hair. "Our lead guitarist, Dylan, introduced us all to Brianna. They dated first but split amicably. Then she took an interest in me. I should have backed off out of solidarity, but the heart just fucking ignores logic sometimes."

"That's your ex-wife, right?" she asks, matter-of-factly.

Nodding, I lean forward, guilt still churning inside. "Dylan gave his blessing but must have secretly harbored some sort of resentment against me because one night we were all out drinking, and he made a crude comment about Brianna. Of course, I couldn't let that stand. I saw red and threw the first punch."

"That's not so uncommon in this business," Mackenzie says, not unkindly. Just telling it how it is. "Internal fighting in bands is par for the course. I can't count the times my guys have been at each other's throats over something stupid."

"That's true, but...God, I was such an idiot..." Shaking my head, I glance at my almost-invisibly damaged knuckles. I see it like a bright neon sign, though I doubt anyone else does. "A full-on brawl exploded, and the whole band got involved. In the chaos, I slammed my fist into a brick wall trying to get to Dylan. Ended up with two broken knuckles and worse. Next day we all sobered up, but the anger stuck around. Accusations were thrown about over who 'ruined everything.' Like my hand, our brotherhood was fractured beyond repair."

I turn my hand palm-up, tracing the faint surgical scar. "I shattered two knuckles and tore a tendon. Had two surgeries, but my hand was never the same after. I couldn't play anymore. Couldn't get the intricate fingerwork back up to speed." Holding my arm up, I show her the faint crookedness of my hand from clumsy healing. "And you know how it ended. Oddly enough, I was the wordsmith, and main lyricist, so they couldn't use my songs once I was gone. They fell apart too. The only silver lining from the brawl was that it put things with Brianna into sharper focus." I can't help the cynical chuckle. "A lot of good that did me in the end."

"Why do you say that?"

As I again stare into the fire, I can still see that fateful night play out again in my mind's eye. The echoes of it haunt me. I try for a sardonic smile that I'm certain resembles more of a grimace at the painful memories this stirs.

Turning, I meet Mackenzie's gaze. "It was a small consolation when everything else crumbled that night. Everything changed with one rash moment. Bri stuck with me, for the most part. But she wanted the rockstar, the lifestyle. When she eventually saw that I wasn't going to be able to give that to her, well...things changed. She changed."

Lapsing into a pained silence, I think of Brianna. In trying to claim love, I'd ultimately destroyed it and so much more in the aftermath. I doomed June and Hayley to a life separate from me.

I doomed everyone.

Mackenzie reaches over and rubs my arm gently,

her voice soft and soothing, yet edged with anger. "Well, if you ask me, it's her fucking loss. Because I think you're pretty great."

I hear her words, but they don't really register. I still mourn the loss of what could have been. What *should* have been. My hand drops heavily to my lap. Even old regrets can still sting.

"It's not entirely her fault, really. I sold her on a dream that I couldn't fulfill. There's no denying that. But I did what I could to stay involved in the business. To be near the limelight I was forced to turn away from. So, I channeled that restless energy into nurturing new talent when Blackmore offered me the scouting gig. It just wasn't enough to hold things together. And now here I am before you, a manager for a band with zero common sense, snowed in at a ski resort in Colorado with no power, probably no festival, and no end to any of it in sight." I give a rueful laugh, heart clenching with how much my life seems to change after split-second decisions.

She doesn't say anything. Just keeps gently rubbing my arm. It's comforting, and just what I need to get the story out. I could feel her compassion and empathy before I said a word. That alone is fucking incredible. *That's* a talent.

But I need to be careful here.

Mackenzie isn't the type of person I want to mess around with just for fun. She deserves more than just a roll in the hay. Even though she says she doesn't want more it's obvious that our connection is deeper than just physical. Whether or not she feels it too I don't know but after everything, I don't want to press the issue and make either of us uncomfortable.

With sex off the table, all that's left is intellectual intercourse, and I don't know that I'm up to the task.

Baring my soul to her like this in the middle of the day is very different than our exchanged confidences at night. There's a glare on every thought and emotion that exposes them more somehow. It's as if when you tell your story at night you can hide behind the shadows, and that can't happen now.

I inhale deeply and push off my knees to stand. "Right. Well, I suppose I should check on the hot water situation. I'm not sure exactly when the power went out, and if there is any hot water left, I'll leave it for you to shower or clean up."

"I could definitely use a shower if there is any."

Squeezing my eyes shut to try to push the picture of Mackenzie naked in the shower out of my brain, I turn and head toward the utility closet. I am the least mechanically inclined person that I know, outside of musical equipment, so what I'm looking for on a hot water heater I have no idea.

As I open the door and look at the contraption, I don't know what I'm looking at, so I cautiously touch the side to see if it's still warm and it seems to be.

"I'm not positive but I believe the water might still be warm, so you should probably take a shower before that changes." I'm still having difficulty not picturing her naked, which is becoming a problem for me.

She stands and grabs her crutches, now adept at maneuvering smoothly with them, and heads toward the bedroom. "Thanks, I'll try to be quick and leave you some."

I'm about to instinctively offer to help but catch myself in time before I embarrass myself all over again. So, I just nod and shut the door to the closet without a word.

With it being so quiet in the cabin, I can hear her moving around, and my dick hardens at the thought of her stripping mere feet away from me. It dawns on me that she might want some clean clothes to change into once she's done with her shower. Once I hear the water start, I enter the bedroom to go through my duffel to see if I have anything she could wear.

Once there, I instantly notice that the door to the bathroom is left open, and while I can't see Mackenzie directly, I do see her reflection in the vanity mirror. Her breathtaking reflection. She's holding on to the wall carefully as the water falls over her, peppering her skin, and droplets giving themselves up to gravity as they slide down her exposed flesh.

As she turns, I get a full view of the breasts I just had in my mouth and my hands not but an hour ago at most, and my fingertips and lips tingle with the desire to touch them again. Even just for a moment. One more moment to carry me through my fantasies with that reality, because right now it still feels like a dream.

I'm frozen, pulse hammering as I drink in elegant curves and planes beaded and glittering. I know I should give her privacy, but I'm transfixed by this unexpected glimpse behind Mackenzie's armor. I'm aching to trail my fingers along her silhouette...that skin... Heat surges lower as my imagination spins wild visions.

Stop it, you perv.

With monumental effort I force rigid limbs into motion, silently pulling the door half-closed. My fists clench, warring with myself. I want Mackenzie, desperately, but not at the cost of her trust. I make myself look away and finish what I came here for. I find a new shirt and pair of shorts that will have to do. I didn't pack much as this festival is only for a few days, and I wasn't expecting to be sharing my wardrobe with anyone. So, the pickings are about to be very slim.

Laying the clothes on the bed for her again and exiting the bedroom, I close the door behind me and try to shutter my mind to the invasive thoughts of everything Mackenzie. If I let them, they will consume me, and I'm not sure I could survive that.

Honestly, I don't know if I'd want to.

CHAPTER 17

WHAT DO I DO

MACKENZIE

Finishing my shower as quickly and as carefully as I can, I exit the bathroom to find that Ian has laid out clean clothes for me. He's got to be running out of his own, so for him to think of me is heartwarming.

Since putting a stop to any thoughts of having sex between us, of course, now it's the only thing I can think about. The memory of his kisses and hands all over me makes me want to take it all back. Just say, *'fuck it,'* and go for the immediate pleasure release that I know would come from it. I don't know what's holding me back, outside of thinking that my judgment is clouded. I'm beginning to question that about myself.

Maybe I'm just afraid.

I think deep down if I let myself, I could really care

about Ian. The complexity of him makes me think it would be easy to love him. I would never be bored. I would always be discovering something new about him that I didn't know before, and that would keep me interested. That's a dangerous trait for me to find in someone else. If someone piques my interest, I tend to go all-in headfirst. I dive into the deep end without taking a deep breath, and the next thing I know I'm drowning.

I could drown in Ian Summer.

I've only been in love, *truly* in love, once in my life. And it was the biggest mistake of my life. It was with a tour manager for a European boy band of all things. And for three months, I thought he was the end-all, be-all, of my world. He was so charming that I willingly handed over my heart. I let him in and let the idea of him, the idea of *us*, take over and take hold. And when I finally gave in and said those three words to him, it changed everything.

Not only did he not say it back, but he acted surprised. He made it seem as if I read into things too deeply. I was seeing things that weren't there. In reality, he was showing me emotions he didn't feel, affections he didn't return, and dreams he never dreamt, but convinced me were real. He made me think that he was in love whether he said the words or not.

He was a fucking liar. And I was a goddamn fool.

No longer am I anyone's fool, and I don't put up

with liars at all. There is no *'Fool me twice'* allowed. Nobody survives the first one. Not with me.

Since then, it's been my mission to never get attached to anyone I'm intimate with. My heart is hidden away and out of reach of anyone who tries to deceive me again. I won't let it happen. Outside of my body, everything is off-limits, and even then, I'm extremely careful.

In my experience, men confuse sex with love. Infatuation with emotion. Attention with attraction. And while sure, the lines can be blurry at times, I make a point to be crystal clear with everyone.

So why am I doubting myself with Ian? Why am I feeling those same stirrings in my chest whenever I see him?

I hold the fresh shirt to my nose and breathe in the scent of him. Alarm bells go off in my head and I'm tempted to ignore them. They're rusty from disuse. Maybe that fact alone should make me pay attention, and it's hard not to.

All I need to do is remember looking at my reflection in the bathroom mirror of the tour bus after that breakup years ago, and the broken look in my eyes. I swore to myself to never feel that way again. No one would ever wield so much power over me or my heart again. Nobody would have so much sway to cripple me with a word, or a dismissal, and I've been determined to keep that promise. That day wrecked me. My armor has since been rebuilt twice as thick, and I dare anyone to be that callous with my bruised spirit again.

But beneath the internal panic at the thought of letting that reinforced guard down stirs an impossible yearning to stop cowing and try trusting whatever this *thing* is between us.

Letting out a long sigh I throw his shirt over my head, wrap myself again in the blanket, and use the crutches to return to the great room of the cabin. Ian is at the sink washing the breakfast dishes and I look out the sliding glass door at the storm. It's relentless, and after so long I'm starting to wonder if it will ever stop.

Placing my fingertips on the glass, the chill seems to crawl up my fingers and into my bones. I think of Billy and everyone else out working in this weather and simultaneously feel bad and grateful. It's people like him that keep the rest of us going. An unsung hero who probably doesn't even know how many people he's helping.

I glance down at the deck piled high with snow, and my eye catches on a dark mound in the corner. I lean in and press my forehead to the glass, my breath steaming the window as I try to see what it could be, but I can't make it out.

"Ian, what is that?" I ask, pointing to the dark spot as he grabs a dish towel to dry his hands and walks over. He leans in close to me to get a better view of whatever it is.

"I don't know," he says squinting. "I think I see fur though. It must be some sort of animal."

"Oh no, do you think it's dead?"

He doesn't even pause to answer and unlocks the door, slides it open, and then in his bare feet trudges through the snow to the pile of fur in the corner. I watch as he cautiously reaches out to touch it and must have some reaction, because he scoops it into his arms, cradles it close to his chest, and hurries back inside.

Shutting the door behind him, I follow as he immediately goes to sit on the hearth by the fire. "What is it? Is it OK?"

"It's a cat, and I think it's still alive but just barely. It's got to be frozen." Holding it close to his chest it still doesn't move, and I worry we may be too late. "I need a towel or a blanket. Something to swaddle it in."

Without thinking twice, I slip the blanket from around my shoulders and help in wrapping the cat who is now trembling and shaking. I don't know if that's a good thing or not. My mind jumps to thoughts that body temperature shouldn't change so quickly but I think in this instance warmth is required.

"Did they cover freezing cats in Boy Scouts? Did you get a badge in that by any chance?" I'm not trying to be funny. As a matter of fact, I'm very serious. I want to be pacing or freaking out, but my crutches thankfully limit my movement.

"Unfortunately, no," he says, finishing wrapping

the cat, leaving its face and pink nose peeking out. Its eyes are still closed and my stomach sinks that we're not doing enough. "I'm just running on instinct here. I've actually never had any pets, so I haven't got the first clue as to how to take care of a healthy cat, let alone one in distress."

His brows furrow with concern as he looks down at the bundle in his arms. He's cradling it like a baby, and seeing him like this, in hero mode yet again, plucks at my heartstrings with such fervor I can almost hear a song.

After giving up my blanket I'm feeling useless to do anything to help, but my racing mind starts expanding its track. "Do you think that was the only one out there? Should we look for others just in case?" I start towards the sliding door to go look for myself when Ian jumps up from the hearth to stop me.

"Here, take it while I go look." And the next thing I know, I'm taking his place by the fire with the cat in my arms while he rushes outside to look for more animals in need.

It's hard to see him in the squall that surrounds him as he digs through the deep snow on the deck. After a few minutes, he's back inside, looking almost as cold as the cat, but I see he doesn't have any more companions this time.

"It appears that the popsicle in your arms is the only nearby victim." He hurries back to the fire, sitting next to me and pulling his feet up to get warm. With his feet bare and being only in a T-shirt and sweats, he's got to be freezing now, too.

"Do you ever take a day off from being a hero?" I ask and take in his snow-dampened hair and flexing biceps as he tries to warm himself. Part of me wants nothing more than to help him, but I choose to keep the cat as my only charge.

A wry smile lifts his expression as he rubs at his feet. "I suppose it's getting to be time for me to reveal my secret superhero identity, isn't it?"

"I knew it. I knew there was something special about you." As soon as I say it, I clamp my lips shut and can feel the embarrassment show on my face. I know that what I said can be taken many ways, and to be honest I probably meant them in all the ways it could be taken. And, as I glance up at him and his soft green eyes that seem to see into my soul, I don't want to take it back.

He *is* special.

His immediate conviction to save this cat, this poor little frozen being, only proves that point.

The question is, what do I do about that?

CHAPTER 18

DEAD TALK

Ian

When Mackenzie gets up to make us both coffees to warm up, I carefully cradle the bundled feline, willing my own warmth deeper into its tiny frozen body. Its tremors slowly subside as I rub its legs through the blanket, its coat drying in silky black tufts against my arms. When she returns, I glance up to catch Mackenzie watching me, cheeks still endearingly flushed from my superhero quip and our close proximity sharing space by the firelight.

"Any sign of consciousness yet in our new friend?" she asks, shifting closer, a tentative smile playing at her lips.

I gently part the blanket near the cat's face. Its breaths seem less labored now, easing out in a reassuring rhythm, but their eyes remain closed. "Doesn't seem ready to wake just yet. But getting stronger, I hope."

Mackenzie lifts a hand, hesitating. "May I?" My heartbeat quickens as her fingers brush mine, contact warming me more than any fire could. I loosen my hold, guiding the cat to settle across both our laps now.

I drink in the care softening Mackenzie's features as she strokes behind its ears. That foreign swell behind my ribs returns. A feeling that's both at once so familiar and brand new in her presence.

Untangling the cloth, I take a brief glance under the blanket and wrap it tightly again. "It looks like our friend here is of the female persuasion."

"Aww, we should give her a name."

Why women feel the need to claim and name every creature is a mystery to me. My daughters do the same thing with their dolls and stuffed animals. They all have names, and even backstories, though I often confuse them. To be fair, they have a lot of dolls and stuffed animals. Their mother tends to spoil them.

And me. I spoil them too.

"I'll let you do the honors," I say, smiling to myself at the thought of Mackenzie ever doing the same when she was little. Far be it from me to get in the way of a naming ceremony.

"Well, she's a black cat, found in white snow..." she

starts, brow creasing as she considers internal options. "She's by herself, but she doesn't look like a stray necessarily."

"What makes you say that?"

She shrugs. "I don't know. I just imagine strays to be more unkempt, or scrawny. She's either taken care of herself, or someone else has. Either way, she's blatantly independent. What about 'Rebel?'"

I scrunch my nose, not keen on that one. "What about 'Mittens?'"

"I thought I was doing the honors," Mackenzie argues, bumping her shoulder playfully into mine.

"Yeah, but look," I say, reaching carefully into the blanket and pulling out a single paw to wave at her. It's white fur pristine. My voice playfully shifts into a higher register, "She's got whittle mittens."

Mackenzie's shoulders drop as she pulls an emotional face. "Aww, look how sweet those little toe beans are." She tickles between the foot pads, and the cat instinctively jerks its paw in response, but still doesn't wake. "I've got it," she announces proudly, sitting up straight. "Stormy."

"Perfect," I say, meeting her violet eyes, and somehow meaning it about more than the cat's new name.

I mean it about her.

Her gaze drops back down to Stormy self-consciously and I have to catch myself. I'm letting

Mackenzie get to me. Deep down I'm wondering if this is all because of our close proximity to each other. I'm allowing my imagination to run recklessly wild here finding meaning behind every single glance from her.

I'm reading into things that probably aren't there.

We're isolated in a remote cabin, bonding through adversity. Of course, sparks might fly, but then they'll most likely fade back to nothing when real life returns. I can't let myself be carried away with what may be nothing more than a fleeting connection forged by these extreme circumstances. No matter how fiercely my foolish heart may want to hope for more. I'm torn between treasuring Mackenzie's company for however long we're going to be stranded, and self-preservation if this is all only whimsy on both of our parts.

I gently extricate Stormy from Mackenzie's lap, moving to settle the slumbering cat on a pillow nearer the fire. Safer to put some physical distance between myself and the intoxicating woman I'm snowbound with before I do something I shouldn't, like beg her not to break whatever spell has been cast on me the last two days.

"There now, steady on," I murmur, adjusting the cat's blankets needlessly, buying time to rein in the embarrassing transparency of my internal thoughts.

Get a grip, man.

I clear my throat gruffly. "What should we try feeding our girl first?" I ask, exhaling slowly and moving to join Mackenzie on the couch while my pulse settles.

Back to practicalities. Probably for the best before I derail this entire train.

CHAPTER 19

CARRION COMFORT

MACKENZIE

After brainstorming with Ian on what to feed a cat, I can't help the huge yawn I attempt unsuccessfully to stifle. I don't know if it's from the excitement of yesterday, which led to my nightmares and sketchy sleep of last night, or the pain medicine, or maybe a combination of all of the above. All I know is I can hardly keep my eyes open. Again.

My leg is propped up on throw pillows and Ian has his arm around me. I nestle against him and do my best to stay awake. We're both watching Stormy with anticipation, willing her to wake up and entertain us.

With the power out and only a sexually suggestive book to read as an activity for the two of us to participate in, we need an outside source of entertainment. But in the downtime waiting for Stormy to grace us with her presence, I don't know if I'll be able to stay awake.

Feeling the steady rise and fall of Ian's chest beneath me, and the calming sound of his breaths, I am quickly asleep.

When I wake up, I notice I have a new friend next to me in the shape of a fur ball that purrs very loudly. As I shift slightly, Stormy raises her head to see what has interrupted her own sleep and glares at me with two different colored eyes, one blue and one green. I whisper an apology and look around for Ian.

It's still light outside but it feels like midafternoon, so I'm hopeful I've only been asleep for a little while. However, I don't see Ian anywhere, but I do hear water running from the direction of the main bedroom and assume he must be taking a shower.

A cold shower.

The cat climbs onto my chest, folding her paws underneath herself as she stares at me, quite content with where she is and apparently not inclined to move anytime soon. Far be it from me to inconvenience this little Princess. From how comfortable she is with me, I get the sense that she's used to humans, and probably belongs to someone. I hope whoever it is doesn't miss her too much and wish we had a way of getting Stormy back home.

"Where did you come from little girl?" I ask, staring back into her intense gaze. "Where do you come from? Where are your people? I bet they miss you."

I don't know whether Stormy understands me or not but her purrs seem to quicken and increase in volume as I talk to her. Maybe she feels the vibration of my voice in my chest and thinks I'm purring back at her.

I don't know how cats work.

"Well, regardless of where you come from, I'm happy that we were able to help you, bring you in, and get you warm, and hopefully fed and watered. Feel free to make yourself comfortable."

Oddly enough I get the feeling that she does understand me and she squints her eyes while still purring. She adds a little stretching of her claws out and in for good measure, kneading her paws into the fabric of Ian's shirt.

Apparently, she's quite content, so I close my eyes again and let the monotonous drone of her rumbling lull me back to sleep.

When I wake again, Stormy is no longer on my chest, and my legs are draped over Ian's lap while he sits on one end of the couch reading a paperback novel of some kind. It must be one of the "regular" books from the nearby shelves.

He looks absorbed in the story, and from what I can see, he's pretty far into the book already. His eyes move quickly down one side then up and down the next before turning the page where he repeats the motion. He goes on like that for quite a while, not noticing that I'm awake yet. I don't know if I've ever seen somebody read that fast before. You always hear about speed reading, but you never see somebody doing it.

I watch in amazement until he's about halfway through the book before I have to shift my weight. My good leg had fallen asleep since I was laying on my side. As I move, he glances over to check on me, and there's something in that small gesture that unwinds something inside me. He didn't look over casually or annoyed that I disturbed his reading. His initial reaction was concern, and checking to see if I was OK.

Maybe I have been alone for too long, or grown too independent to care, or just not paying attention, but I can't remember the last time somebody looked at me just to make sure I was alright. Even as I think this, I know how sad it sounds in my head. I don't consider myself a nominee for a pity party, but in all honesty, maybe I should throw one for myself.

If there are other people in the world like Ian, that would look at me that way, then maybe I've been missing out on quite a lot. But then, why should I have to keep missing out? Why shouldn't I let myself feel whatever I want to feel, or do whatever I want to do with another consenting adult?

What is finally eroding the last of my restraint? Is this cozy isolation from real life, allowing our true selves to emerge? Is my near brush with mortality making me question what really matters? Or is it just the crazy magnetic pull of this incredible man who somehow sees the real me that I hide from almost everyone?

Between watching him read, the way he's staring at me right now with a slight glint in his eyes like he knows exactly what I'm thinking, and every other amazingly fantastic thing he's done the last two days, I think it's about time I gave in.

I sit up briefly and pluck the book from his hands, dog ear the page he was on, and toss it on the coffee table.

He inhales an audible gasp and covers his mouth with a hand. "You blasphemer, you."

Grabbing his hands, I pull him toward me as I lay back. "I guess I've been a very bad girl then, huh?"

He stretches himself over top of me with a sly smile, "I guess you have." Hovering over me while holding himself up on his elbows, he studies my face. I can see the question in his eyes, the desire that matches my own. And I want nothing more than to give in to it.

"Well, what are you going to do about it?" I ask, dragging a nail down the side of his neck. The degree of satisfaction I get when he squirms under my touch is entirely too much. I love that a little touch like that from me can get that kind of a reaction from him. And that's not all I feel as his growing erection presses against me.

There's still a question in his eyes and he seems to be hesitating despite his obvious interest in taking this farther. "Are you sure you want me to do something about this reprehensible behavior? I'm not doing a damn thing until you say it's OK."

If there was something more perfect that he could have said right then, I have no clue what it could be, because that was exactly the right thing to say. Not only is this man hot, but he's principled.

Fucking hell.

"Oh, I am absolutely sure I want you to do something about it," I say pulling him down to nip at his bottom lip. In that same motion, I grind up against his hard cock feeling myself warm in anticipation. "And you'd better do it soon."

He doesn't say anything in response but takes my mouth with his, a growl rumbling low in his throat as his tongue thrashes against mine. The ties on my braid come undone, and he runs his nimble fingers through my hair. He wraps it around his fist and gently pulls, forcing my head back and exposing my neck.

As his mouth glides along my jaw and down my throat, his teeth graze and bite ever so lightly with just the right combination of pleasure and pain. The mix of heat from his wet tongue and coolness from the air of his breath against my delicate skin sends me into a frenzy. I have to be careful with my leg, but I'm doing what I can to make room for him.

Reaching down, I grab the hem of his shirt and

drag it slowly up his torso, watching his tattoos flex and dance along with our heavy breathing. Before he returns to kiss me, he removes my shirt and drops it on top of his own. When he sees I'm not wearing a bra he cups both of my breasts in his hands, massaging them with something close to devotion in his eyes. Feathering his touch along my nipples with his thumb, his gaze grows ravenous, and he leans in to greedily suck one while roughly teasing the other.

I drag my nails down his back as he sears my skin with blistering intensity, savoring the taste of me as his kisses travel across my stomach and past my navel. My thighs are already trembling as he carefully removes the rest of my clothes, and the awareness of him concentrating on my entire body, which is now exposed, builds a craving so deep within me that I can't take much more.

"Look at you." His breath is coming out in shuddering waves. "Look at this perfection, all for me. Is this for me too?" he asks, running a tantalizing finger through my center causing my hips to buck in response.

I grope for him again, but he slides down the couch and out of reach as he traces kisses up my thighs. The aching between my legs builds even more when he reaches my core. Rolling his tongue over my clit with firm and demanding strokes, the throbbing pleasure becomes overwhelming as the intensity crests.

My fingers rush through his hair, and I don't know

whether I'm trying to hold him in place or push him away, maybe both. All I know is the sensation flooding through me causes me to cry out in ways I never have before. He barely touched me, and yet I practically came instantly as soon as he did.

"That's it. That's my girl," he whispers, kissing his way back up my body, the vibrations in my blood-stream still simmering beneath the surface. "That's what I wanted to hear."

"What's that?" I ask my breathing still labored. My fingers are still reaching for his cock but he's deftly avoiding me. It's getting frustrating.

I can feel him smile against my neck as he says, "My name."

Did I call out his name? I don't even remember. I was so lost to the sensation of bliss coursing through me, that I could have been speaking in tongues for all I know.

"Why won't you let me touch you?" I ask, tugging on his hair so he'll look at me. "I want to return the favor."

"So, I just did you a favor?" His sly smile barely has time to register before his mouth is on mine, the salt of my own skin, my own essence, coming back to me.

In coming up to kiss me, however, he brought himself within my reach, and I take advantage of it, reaching into his pants and taking hold of his smooth shaft. His breath hitches as I glide my fist up and down, clutching his thick erection with the same urgency he paid to my clit.

"Come for me baby," I whisper hoarsely, feeling every single one of his muscles tense at my words. I almost feel drunk with power knowing that my touch arouses the quickening within him. "Let it go. Let yourself go."

"Fuck. Christ. Mackenzie." He buries his face into the crook of my neck as he surges into my hand. Erupting on a groan. Hot and wet and sexy as fuck.

Carefully he settles over me, still breathless and panting, and I wrap an arm around him. He's still semi-erect and I haven't let him go yet, so I swirl his tip with my thumb, feeling him quiver with each brush of skin.

"You need to stop doing that, Mackenzie. Or I'm not going to be responsible for what I do next."

I grip him tighter. "All I hear is blah blah blah, challenge, blah blah blah." I can't help the smile that comes along with my words.

Suddenly, to my left is a small black furry face with two different colored eyes that are very curious about the current goings on in the room. Ian sees her too and starts chuckling.

"I suppose this is very impolite of us to do in front of our new guest." He pushes up onto his elbows and gazes down at me, ignoring Stormy. "Thank you, Mackenzie." He brushes his lips against mine and repeats the phrase, "Thank you."

Something about him saying those words, in that way, at this moment, unlocks something in my chest. I don't know if it's the look in his eyes, or the tone of his voice when he says it, but something has shifted. It might have just shifted inside of me, and not him, but things are somehow different now.

I only hope it's a good thing.

After I take a shower and cobble together a semblance of dinner for us, Mackenzie leans against me, leg propped up, contentedly petting Stormy who is decidedly comfortable in her new surroundings. Electricity still feels like it's crackling through my limbs where they are entwined with Mackenzie's. But it's still the only electricity in the cabin. If not for the fire, we'd be sitting in the dark.

"She likes you," I murmur, reaching over to give Stormy a scritch behind the ear.

"Yeah, I don't know why," she says dourly. "Me and pets don't usually vibe."

I can't imagine anyone disliking Mackenzie. "How so?"

She sighs, continuing to drag her nails lightly through the cat's fur. "I'm not sure. Maybe because

I've never had pets. I don't know how to interact with them. And it's not like there's a lot of opportunity on the road, outside of an occasional venue or radio station mascot dog or something."

"Well, maybe you should reconsider. Stormy seems to have put some trust in you."

"I don't know," she says doubtfully. "I mean, I've seen a lot of snakes on the road. You'd be surprised how many bands bring snakes on tour. It's almost weird."

She's not wrong. I've seen my fair share of all sorts of snakes in my travels from venue to venue. "And how do the snakes treat you?"

Holding out her right hand, she points to a very intricate red and orange snake tattoo that wraps around her middle finger. "I got this one in honor of Betty."

"And who is Betty?" It sounds familiar to me for some reason, but I can't place it.

She chuckles to herself. "Betty is Trent from Incendiary Ink's corn snake. She's a sweetheart."

Reptiles, or anything cold-blooded aren't exactly my cup of tea, but I'm intrigued. "What makes a snake a sweetheart, exactly?"

"Well, in Betty's case, she would seek me out if I was around. She liked crawling into my shirt and tickling me with her tongue."

Of course, that gets an immediate dick twitch, and I can't help sliding a hand under her shirt. Her smooth skin is warm and inviting. "Betty and I are a lot alike it seems..."

She laughs and jerks away, obviously ticklish. Stormy is startled and bolts to hide somewhere, giving me more room to roam. I take advantage of the opportunity and grab Mackenzie's waist, pulling her closer despite her veiled protests. Her laughter dies as she gives in and melts into me, returning my kisses with an enthusiasm I didn't expect, but that I love.

Before it escalates to another level, one that I can't tear my mind from, I reluctantly pull away. Breathing heavily, we share a gaze so intense that I swear she can read my mind or see into my soul. I feel exposed and vulnerable, and I don't know if I like it. I'm not used to it.

Even with Brianna, I never felt this way. Everything with her was on the surface level, where I knew where I stood. This is so different. This, whatever *this* is, is tapping into emotions I didn't know I possessed. Feelings I don't know what to do with.

How the hell did we get here so quickly? Not quite two days ago, she was an intriguing industry peer. Now I'm bloody besotted like some teenager after one mind-blowing shag.

No. It's not just that. It's not just physical. And I know it.

And it bothers the fuck out of me.

"Sorry," I mutter, pulling away and trying to compose myself. If left to my own devices, I'd ravage

Mackenzie all over again right here and now. But I can't do that. I need to find a way to control myself around her. How I go about that, I have no idea, but I have to figure it out. Otherwise, this can go balls up in a heartbeat for both of us.

I really don't want to hurt her.

"You okay?" she asks, concerned.

"I am tickety-boo, as my Nan used to say." I force a smile. "That means 'good.'"

Mackenzie nods and seems to understand the line in the sand I'm drawing between us for now. Of course, she does. Leaning back into me as she was before, the cat must have been watching as she jumps right back onto Mackenzie's chest and starts kneading her paws, the low rumble of her purr filling the silent air.

I grab my discarded paperback from the coffee table and flip to the dog-eared page where I left off, throat tight. This is killing me. Mackenzie has bared her trust in me, but I still hide truths about myself that could ruin this chemistry combusting between us.

The longer I go without telling her about June and Hayley's existence, the worse it'll bite both of us when she eventually learns I held back. But confessing now feels like it would be destined to smother this fragile relationship kindling between us. And she's made it perfectly clear how she feels about a family.

And that's not the only reason I hesitate to tell her about my daughters. It already feels too late. I've already betrayed whatever trust she's placed in me. Lies by omission are still lies, aren't they? Or am I getting way ahead of myself?

Maybe what's happening between us is absolutely nothing. Just a fling. Nothing serious. We're just killing time in a weird situation as two consenting adults who happen to be attracted to each other.

And get along like a house on fire.

And understand each other without explanation.

And...*fuck*.

That's not to say Mackenzie feels the same way about me. She's said nothing, and really given no solid indication that whatever's going on is anything more than a casual tryst for her. I'm not the only one here, acting on impulse. She is too.

Is this just temporary insanity between us? Convenience and impulse bonding us with little substance beneath?

I stare blindly at the book's pages, not seeing the words, gut churning. I've backed myself into a fucking corner here. But what can I do? Destroy a fragile bond too intoxicating to imagine over things not said? Or pray my porous excuses to myself hold water a little longer.

I don't like any of my options. Not anymore.

And I've done this to myself.

C urled in one of Ian's borrowed sweatshirts, I cradle a steaming mug of freshly made hot cocoa, pleasantly worn out. Stormy dozes comfortably by the hearth, tail flicking occasionally in a kitten dream. The quiet feels like a balm, only the soft crackle of logs breaking the silence once in a while. It's almost as though we're living in one of those hours-long YouTube videos with a 'snow cabin scene' it's so surreal.

When did I last allow myself to enjoy so much stillness? Years maybe, if ever. I'm always rushing headlong onto the next crisis. I don't take time like this for myself.

Ever.

Yet now, barricaded by snowdrifts with Ian, my typical anxiety tingles surprisingly deep beneath my skin. It's not just under the surface threatening to overtake me. Laughter slips out easier now than it ever has before. The peaceful lulls only amplify that foreign lightness fizzing through my veins. It's making me feel like a completely different person.

And it's not all bad.

I don't know if I could get used to this on a permanent basis, but for now, it's exactly what I needed. It only took a ski accident, broken bone, hospital visit, and blizzard to make it happen, but beggars can't be choosers, I guess. Oh, and an amazing and totally hot rescuer, too. I can't forget that.

Who could forget Ian, really? And why would anyone want to?

My gaze catches on him organizing provisions across the room in the kitchen area. I should feel uneasy at this unfamiliar calm, like waiting for the other shoe to drop, as always seems to happen. Instead, an affectionate warmth blooms in my chest seeing his perpetually mussed bedhead cowlick. My lips quirk as he fumbles a box of pasta before righting it, ears reddening. When did I start trusting someone could accept my thorns as readily as my petals? When did I start trusting him?

He's been so open with me, and so honest, it feels like we could tell each other anything. His opening up to me about what happened with his band, and with his ex-wife, showed me a different side of him. A complex side that I knew was there somewhere but finally made itself known.

Everyone has demons. Reasons and circumstances that make people the way they are. We all are brought up differently, grow differently, rebel differently, and end up being some sort of mash-up of all of it. And each hurt caused by those things heals differently too. It's that scar tissue that hardens us to the world around us. Makes us hide ourselves away.

I feel like I'm getting to see beyond those layers with Ian. And I like what I see. He's decent. He's vulnerable. He's principled. And, he cares.

I only have to look at Stormy warming herself by the fire to see a glimpse of that. How many people would run into a blizzard only half-dressed to save a defenseless animal in distress? Or stop to help a stranger on a ski slope obviously in need? Unfortunately, these days, not that many. People are too afraid of repercussions to do anything brave anymore. Nobody wants to stick their neck out or get involved. They're too worried about themselves to try to help.

Not Ian.

My mind eventually drifts to the hotel and the festival. Murderous Crows will manage without my constant oversight, I concede to myself begrudgingly. I wouldn't dare say that to them, however. But, I've seen an evolution in every one of them, including Skyler who's only been with us for a relatively short time. It's strange to be so needed for so long to now feel almost like an afterthought. I know that's not the case, by the sheer amount of work I do, but it's changed over the last couple of years.

Andy's death changed everything for all of us. To be honest, I don't know where we'd be if the accident never happened. I don't know that it wouldn't have taken another accident, or tragedy to pull things into perspective for everyone. Not that it was a good thing. Far from it. I miss him every single day, and even just thinking about him now makes me tear up. I think he would be proud of how far we've all come. How much we've achieved both individually and as a family.

"You alright, love?" Ian's concerned voice pulls me from my inner thoughts. He sits next to me and gently wipes tears from my cheeks that I didn't realize I'd let fall.

"What? Oh." Suddenly, I'm self-conscious, and let out a nervous laugh. I give him a sad smile. "Yeah. Tickety-boo."

CHAPTER 22

MORE THAN THIS

IAN

W e both sit in silence for a long while, getting lost in our own thoughts as we're hypnotized by the dancing flames of the fire. Despite the raucous noise in my head, it's a comfortable silence. The ease between us feels supernatural.

Mackenzie breaks through with a loud yawn and stretches languidly like Stormy did not minutes ago. Her hidden feline nature cutting through.

"Well, I should let you get some rest," I say, standing to help her up. "Do you need anything? A pain pill? Assistance of any kind?" My dirty mind and I leave the door open for *any* possibility.

She shakes her head, holding a hand out for me to pull her up. "No. I think I'm okay." She starts toward the bedroom, maneuvering without her crutches now.

"But..." She bites her lip alluringly if a bit unsure. "You could maybe stay. With me."

My pulse trips over the speed bumps of her words. Does she mean...? No, best not to assume. Still, hope springs stubbornly eternal. I can barely get out one word, "Sorry?"

Pink blooms on her cheeks but she shrugs with affected nonchalance. "I mean, if you want. You know, in case I have bad dreams again." Her eyes glint warmly through her played-off excuse. "Strictly for nightmare prevention purposes, of course."

I can't restrain my ridiculous grin even as warning sirens blare distantly in my mind. "Of course. Well, I can't argue with medical rationale like that, can I?"

Following her into the bedroom, I start the literal fire in the fireplace while she gets herself ready for bed. Then I head back out to the great room to extinguish the fire in that one and to make sure Stormy is taken care of for the rest of the night. As I scatter the embers and wait for the ashes to smother any remaining flames I think about Mackenzie, and what might lie ahead this evening.

Maybe I'm assuming too much, and she really means for us just to sleep, which is a perfectly legitimate possibility. She is still healing, after all.

My raging hormones on the other hand have other ideas. I've thought of nothing else since this afternoon. And the taste of her, even though fresh in my memory, has haunted me these last hours with her sitting right beside me.

It takes a while for the embers to completely die down enough for me to think it's safe to leave for the night, and when I do finally make it to bed I find Mackenzie sound asleep.

I have to smile to myself ruefully because it seems like my libido rarely catches a break. Tonight is apparently no different. But it is what it is, and I'll just have to deal with it.

So, I slide under the covers, and, even in her sleep, Mackenzie is drawn to me. Her warm body presses against my chilled skin, and it takes all my resolve not to wake her. As she leans against me, her hand slides around my waist, pulling me to her. I go willingly, wrapping my arms securely around her, hoping to ward off any bad dreams she might have. Trying to ease her subconscious mind that I'm here and will take care of her.

The thought of taking care of someone, anyone, again, while daunting, is remarkably satisfying. I don't know if it's the alpha caveman inside of me that wants to be the protector, or the defender, or what, but I like the idea of taking care of Mackenzie. It's been obvious throughout our stay that she doesn't normally allow that, or doesn't like it, but that doesn't mean she doesn't need it once in a while either.

Everyone needs somebody to take care of them occasionally, and if I can be that for her in her time of need, then I'm happy to do it. Maybe *especially* because she doesn't want it. There are a lot of times someone is defensive, overly independent, or outwardly strong when inside they are only that way because they feel they need to be, they *have* to be. They don't know that it doesn't always have to be that way.

I know I'm like that quite often, too. I think that's why Mackenzie and I get along so well. We would both rather figure things out on our own than ask for help.

Sometimes that's a great way to be because you learn new things, and once you've learned that thing, you can expand on it and create something else. But sometimes you get in your own way, and your stubbornness becomes a downfall. I haven't decided yet whether or not Mackenzie allowing me to help her is going to be *my* downfall or not. That's yet to be seen.

Running my fingers gently through her long hair, I listen to her soft rhythmic breathing, wondering what, if anything, can ever come of this. In my heart and mind, I already know I've fucked this up by keeping secrets. But God damn, the stubborn part of me wants to think, wants to believe, that if whatever's happening between us is real, it could overcome something like that. I know it's foolish and selfish, and all of the above list of bad things, but I still have a stupid wish that miracles can happen.

Maybe for once, they can happen to me.

After several minutes, and just as I am about to doze off, mostly out of exhaustion from beating myself up, Mackenzie seems to stir in my arms. She makes a small noise in her throat as her hand slowly skims across my bare chest up to my neck. As I look down, I see that her eyes are open, and in the dim firelight dancing across her face, I see a desire that matches my own. Just the barest of touches from her, and I'm thrown into a tailspin.

She pulls me into a soft and lingering kiss that is so gentle and meaningful that any defenses I may have had crumble away under the avalanche of emotions that run through me. If I had any doubt that Mackenzie felt about me the way I'm feeling about her they are instantly vanquished.

Cupping the back of her head and being careful of her leg I deepen the kiss trying to express to her that same exact notion, that I'm in this with her. Her body reacts to my touch, pressing against me, and my hand slides down to her hip, grabbing the flesh as I grind my aching cock against her. The sparks radiating at every point our bodies touch start to spread fire in my veins.

She takes my hand and guides it to the junction of her thighs, and I find her bare with nothing on but my T-shirt. My fingers find her saturated and she rocks slowly into my hand, groaning softly as her kisses find their way to my throat. My hard-on strains, even more, when her fingers stroke my length with a feather-light touch that leaves me throbbing for more.

"What about your leg?" I ask softly, not wanting to make a single move that would hurt her.

"What leg?" she asks, shaking her head with a sexy grin before pulling me back into a kiss.

Spurred on, I move to carefully settle on top of her, I entwine both of our hands, pressing them into the mattress to keep her from pushing me over the edge too soon. I want to simmer in this euphoria as long as possible. Pulling her T-shirt up with my teeth, and exposing her breasts, I devote time to tantalizing each nipple, possessing them with searing sweeps of my mouth. Her pelvis lifts, searching for a glimpse of friction with every flick of my tongue.

I follow the path of her tattoos, drawing heated kisses along the outline of the roses etched into her side, tracing possessive lines with my teeth on the shadows of the dragon on her hip. And sketching my own portrait with a brush of my lips on her inner thigh, reveling in the quivering of her muscles as she spreads herself for me. Her fingers cling to mine, trembling along with her body as my mouth plants lingering swirls on her already swollen sex.

As I tease and graze her most sensitive spot, she rips her hands from mine, threads her fingers in my hair, and pulls me up to face her. Her hooded eyes are blazing as she says, "Inside me. I want you inside me this time. Now."

I search her face, making sure this isn't a dream. And by the lustful glint in her eyes, I see that we're both of the same mind. Covering her mouth with mine, I press my erection against her communicating my agreement.

But I want to take my time. I want this to be special. I want this to last.

The intensity of the kiss leaves me breathless as the exquisite sensation of our connection brings every nerve ending into indescribable awareness. The thundering of my pulse and the heating of my blood is divine torture.

Mackenzie nudges into me, her nails clutching my shoulders almost painfully, with a desperation so feverish I can't deny her any longer. I drag myself away only momentarily to grab a condom, and once it's in place I retrace my steps along the dragon, and the roses, across her breasts, along her collarbone, and to her throat beneath her ear.

Once I reach the area of her neck that I know drives her crazy, I center myself and sink into her with excruciating slowness, savoring the melting of our bodies together. The sweet groan Mackenzie exhales as I delve into her echoes in my veins. Thrusting deliberately and steadily I raise myself to gaze into her stunning eyes, the intensity between us building with every breath.

When I start to feel weightless, and her muscles start to tense around me, I fight with myself not to speed up, not to be aggressive. Instead, I concentrate on her reactions with each movement. Bearing down as she sinks her teeth into my shoulder, her walls shuddering around me, I allow myself to surge in, anchoring myself as I pulsate and throb inside her. The cresting of pleasure is nearly overwhelming.

I collapse on her chest carefully, her accelerated heartbeat loud beneath my ear. I don't think I've ever had a stronger orgasm in my life. I can still feel it like a quake rumbling over my entire body. It's magical.

She traces lazy circles on the sweat-dampened skin of my back as we lay still, neither of us saying a word. Probably too dumbfounded to think of any. At least, I am. I don't know that I'll ever recover from this.

"Thank you," she whispers into my hair, echoing my sentiment from earlier back to me, and my heart clenches.

I don't have words to respond. Even if I did, I don't have a voice to convey them. I'm floating and sinking at the same time, being pulled in all directions simultaneously.

Being torn apart.

L ost in the delirious afterglow, I trail lazy fingers down Ian's spine as he struggles not to flinch or react, failing miserably. The golden firelight paints shifting shadows across his features, displaying his satisfaction. Outside, the snow continues falling as we hover in our private little world.

I must touch a particularly sensitive spot as Ian jerks in response, and I muffle a giggle into his hair. "Now who's ticklish?"

"Not ticklish, just sensitive," he protests with a chuckle, kissing my neck.

I muffle a giggle into his hair and inhale contentedly when suddenly every light explodes on, appliances whirring to life, and a radio playing loudly in the other room. We jolt upright in surprise.

"What fresh hell?" Ian scowls adorably, squinting at the brightness of the room. "What idiot left all the lights on? Wait, don't answer that..."

"I wouldn't dare."

"Bloody hell, the power's back." Ian tosses the covers aside, announcing the obvious as he hurriedly steps into his boxers. I have to bite my tongue before I can make a sarcastic reply.

He hurries to the kitchen area to shut off the radio, and I limp after him. Despite this positive turn of events, dread creeps in that this little paradise that we've found ourselves in is well and truly over. The thought makes my stomach tighten with disappointment.

Scrambling towards where our dead phones lie abandoned on the counter, he looks around, "Here, help me gather cables, let's get these charging straight away..."

I try to shake off the feeling as Ian sets the phones up to charge, and ominous possibilities start to plague me over what emergencies we might have missed while we were blissfully ignorant in our little cocoon.

"Is there service?" I ask, only partly wanting to know the answer.

We both lean over the counter to watch the screens in anticipation as power slowly trickles into the phones, lighting them up one by one. Then they both erupt with notifications and we each grab our own to see what we've been missing.

Mine are mostly from people checking in on me to see how I'm doing.

> SKYLER: Hey Mac. So sorry about your accident! I feel so bad. Call me when you get this. Let me know you're ok. All is good in birdland. Don't worry about us. (tho I know you will) :D

> CHELSIE: Hey chick. I just saw the huge storm hitting where you're at. Let me know you at least made it in okay. Btw, Jett misses his aunt. Can't wait to see you for Christmas. We all miss you. ~C.

> REMY: Hey. Sky told us about your accident. Just checking on you.

> SKYLER: Checking on you again. Haven't heard from you. Hope you're ok. Is it true you're with Ian? Ooh la la. j/k. maybe.

> CHELSIE: Woman. Text me. Now I'm getting worried. I saw that the festival might get canceled. Let me know you're safe. Love you. ~C.

It goes on with more texts, and growing concern from everyone as I wasn't able to respond. I check my email to find messages from both Blackmore and the festival promoters.

FROM: Eliza.Kerr@blackmorerec.com
TO: Mackenzie.Roberts@blackmorerec.com

SUBJECT: Aspen Alive Festival

Hi Mac,

I just heard about your accident and the storm from Skyler, and wanted to see how you were faring. Hopefully, it's not too bad, and you're up and about in no time. I tried calling, but understand that cell service might be sketchy.

Luckily, Ian Summer is also in town with Chaos Fuel and should be able to give you an assist with the festival. However, since you do the job of three managers, he may need some direction with the production side of things should it come to it. I think you two know each other, and you should have his number, but if you don't, it's...

Ha, 'I think you two know each other.' Oh, Eliza, if you only knew how well we actually do.

I glance up to share the email with Ian and find his back turned to me, and he's rubbing at his neck anxiously.

"Is everything okay?" I ask, now worried that his messages weren't as innocuous as mine.

He looks up at me blankly, seeing right through me momentarily before focusing. "Huh? Oh, sorry. Yeah. It's just a lot..."

"That doesn't sound good. Anything I can help with?"

His eyes widen briefly before flashing down to his phone again as he paces away. "No. No. Nothing I can't handle," he mutters, unplugging his phone and heading towards the study. "I'm sure you've got your own issues to deal with. I need to make some calls..."

Before I can respond any further or remind him that it's 2:30 a.m. in the morning, he shuts the door, leaving me to exchange glances with Stormy, who has jumped onto the stool next to me. Her beautiful eyes are curious about the sudden bustle and noise.

Maybe I should feel offended that he's shutting me out of whatever fire he's putting out, but I know how it is. Sometimes you need to be in private to raise the hell you need to.

I reach over and scratch behind her ear with a shrug. "Men are weird, right?"

Her only response is a slow blink as she starts to purr.

She agrees.

CHAPTER 24

PLASTIC HEART

IAN

I shut the study door, my pulse spiking at the string of demanding voicemails and texts from Brianna blinking insistently on my phone screen. Bracing myself, I hit call back, fervently praying Mackenzie can't overhear through walls.

My ex launches in without preamble. "There you are. Why haven't you answered about Christmas plans? I've been trying to reach you for days."

I pinch my nose, letting her diatribe wash over me. Of course, she assumes I'll drop everything as soon as she snaps her fingers. While she's not a completely horrible person, she'll also never change.

"For your information, I'm currently snowed in and have been without power or cell service until just now."

She sighs as if she doesn't believe me. "It doesn't

snow in LA, Ian. I'm not stupid. You can just say you've hooked up with someone, you know."

I grit my teeth, trying desperately not to fall into old patterns of arguments with her. "I'm not in LA, Brianna, I'm in Aspen if you must know. We were hit with a blizzard."

She's silent for a moment as if having to adjust her attitude takes time. "Oh. Well. I need you to come get the girls for the holidays. Axel is taking me to Tenerife for Christmas."

The nerve of her thinking I'll ferry our daughters back and forth to her whims despite the holiday only being a week away is typical Brianna. The thought of seeing my daughters in person again after so long is beyond tempting, but being ordered to do it has me bristling. Plus, I don't even know if I could given the band's touring schedule, which isn't etched in my brain yet.

"The girls would love to see you, wouldn't you girls?" She holds the phone out and I can hear my girls cheer excitedly in agreement at the idea. My chest tightens with guilt at the sound of their voices. Exactly what their mother intended. "See? They miss their father."

"Brianna enough," I hiss once she pauses for air. "You can't just announce you won't be around and expect me to collect the girls last minute from the other side of the world. I don't even know where I'll be on Christmas. And, how dare you--"

She interrupts me and her tone turns icy. "Your mother already agreed that it's a wonderful idea, and she can watch them some of the time. But apparently, I have to tell you since you clearly can't be bothered to call your own flesh and blood..."

My chest tenses further at the unfair accusation, breath coming sharp and fast as my blood pressure rises. But before I can spit the furious rebuttal clogging my throat, a muffled sound from the other room reminds me to lower my voice again. I curse internally. Nothing about this conversation can reach Mackenzie's ears. Not now. Not yet.

Brianna and my mother now have me cornered, and I don't have a lot of options. My girls are my priority and leaving them with my mother is simply out of the question. The last thing I need is another person bad-mouthing me to them. I'm sure they get enough of that from Bri.

Sighing, I make a split-second decision. "Fine. Let me figure out what's going on here, and I'll get back to you later today or tomorrow, alright? Just don't promise them anything yet. Please."

I have to add that last part because she's also been known to build up expectations in my daughters that I have no way of living up to. Which makes me constantly out to be the bad guy.

"Oh, I won't," she says, her tone sickly sweet, and I don't buy it for a minute.

"Did you at least get the presents I sent for them

already?" I ask, knowing she did because I saw that she signed for them. But coming from me, God only knows what she did with them.

"I did, but I haven't looked at them yet." Now that she's getting her way, she sounds distracted and bored with our conversation. *Too bad*.

"Well, they're not for *you* to look at. They're for June and Hayley," I say, starting to pace again. The back of my mind is already leaping ahead to the next steps I'll need to take to get to London.

"I know..."

This is useless. "Right. Well, I'll be in touch," I announce, hanging up. Right when I do, my phone runs out of the limited juice it got during the brief second it charged.

I toss my phone on the desk, and go back to pacing, raking my fingers through my hair. This is a mess. This is a *fucking* mess. How the hell am I going to handle this now?

Ian stays sequestered in the study for so long that eventually, my curiosity overrides my patience. Limping to the closed door, I rap gently. "Everything okay in there?"

A lengthy silence follows, ambiguous noises rustling on the other side. Finally, Ian emerges looking distinctly more ragged than when he slipped off, his weak smile feels forced.

My brows knit in concern, hand trailing down his arm. "That was an awfully long business call for 3:00 a.m. I heard voices raised at one point. Is there trouble with the bands back at the hotel I should know about?"

"What's that, love? Oh no, just uh..." He glances away, obviously still distracted, clearing his throat. "Just a minor scheduling kerfuffle is all. Riders are not being upheld properly, and shit like that. You know us musicians, everything's a fucking crisis." His chuckle sounds strained, and I don't like this sudden change in him. He grabs his phone from the desk and takes it back into the kitchen.

My eyes narrow, my pulse picking up. Riders are always a battle, but I've never seen such caginess from Ian before. And after our intimacy just a little while ago, this shift feels awfully severe like the blizzard wind still whistling through cracks in the windows.

"Are you sure everything's alright?" I press gently. "I know I was...distracted earlier but please don't shut me out from issues I should hear about, or things I can help with. We're in this together."

"Don't fret yourself over my musicians throwing tantrums." Ian pulls me into a loose embrace. "I've got the mess in hand. There's nothing for you to worry over."

As he turns, my gaze catches on his inert phone abandoned mid-counter.

"Your cell died?"

He pauses, his smile rueful. "Unfortunately, yes. I only had a few minutes of juice left. But the issue with the other openers is sorted now at least."

I nod slowly, details not quite adding up. But suspicion breeds assumptions I remind myself. I need to stop thinking that way, especially about Ian. "Well, if you need help when our phones are fully functional again, I hope you know you can include me. We're partners on this festival ride after all."

Ian's expression softens as he draws me in, thumb grazing my cheek. "Of course, love. You'll be my first stop whenever things get thorny again." The contact comforts me despite the lingering sense of disconnect when he pulls away towards the bedroom. "Shall we try for a bit more rest at least?"

I force a brighter tone to temper the disquiet left swirling in my heart in his wake. "If you insist. But don't think you're off the hook that easily, mister."

I STIR TO THE RUMBLE OF MALE VOICES BY THE FRONT DOOR. Forcing my bleary eyes open, I recognize Billy's Santa Claus tenor mingling with Ian's familiar lilt. I grimace up at the ceiling. Our snowbound days of blissful isolation are apparently numbered now, if not entirely over since it sounds like Billy says that plows have carved paths back to reality.

My pulse stutters at the prospect. Isn't this what I ultimately wanted? To get back to the bands, to my responsibilities? My job?

I don't want to go. Not yet.

Why does the mere thought of venturing back into the real world cause an almost violent reluctance? Just the idea of leaving this place, our sanctuary, makes me hesitant. I cuddle into Stormy who has apparently joined me in my late morning sleep, her soft fur a suddenly-needed comfort.

A gentle rapping sounds at the bedroom door before it cracks open to reveal Ian's kind eyes, an unreadable cautiousness lurking just beneath.

"Good morning. Our intrepid rescuer Billy has braved fresh powder to check in on us. The roads are finally clear enough should we wish to...reassess our lodging arrangements. I just need to call him for a ride."

The unspoken question hovers anxiously between us, and I can't tell from his expression how he wants things to go now. Is it possible to live in this dream for just a few stolen hours more? Or do we need to submit to the real world remorselessly calling us back? I waver internally, wishing desperately I knew what Ian wanted.

But instead of wondering, I gather the nerve to ask him outright. "What do you think? Should I head back now that it's clear?" My throat tightens as I ask, suddenly afraid that we're not on the same page.

He moves to sit on the foot of the bed, reaching out to pet Stormy and avoids my eyes. "That's your decision, Mackenzie. I can't make that for you."

His expression is unreadable, and it's frustrating as hell. "But what do *you* want me to do? Do you want me to leave?"

Ian's head snaps up, and he finally meets my gaze,

his green eyes flashing. "Of course not. I'd love nothing more than for us to stay here together, holed away from the outside world. But I know how important your job is to you and understand if you want to get back to it."

While my heart warms that he does want me to stay, he does have a point. I do want to do my job. At least, as much as I can given my current state.

"What's the word from the promoters? Is the show still on?" That will help me decide what to do. If there's no show, and it's just paperwork and insurance cleanup, I can stay here. But if the festival is still going to happen, then I should probably get a move on back to where I'll be most useful.

His shoulders slump as he releases my gaze as if he knows my decision. "According to Billy, the weather is supposed to break this afternoon. And the promoters say the show is still going forward tomorrow."

My heart sinks, and I instantly feel guilty. I shouldn't be upset that the show is going to happen. I should be happy. It's what we came here for after all.

An idea hits me. "Why don't you come stay at the hotel? With me?" A spark of excitement at the idea runs through me.

"Unfortunately," he frowns, returning his attention to Stormy, "this one still needs to be tended to. Billy doesn't know of anyone missing a cat. And, well, he apparently knows everything about and everyone in this town. The people that live here permanently, which are few and far between, aren't missing her. I can't just leave her."

The kindness in his tone as he looks at her sweetly melts my heart. Of course, he wouldn't abandon Stormy. Not like I'm apparently about to. Something in me tugs at the thought of leaving both of them, but I also know myself. I won't be satisfied hiding away here, no matter how much I want to. The old pull of my job feels wrong somehow, but it's still there. Old habits die really hard.

"That's right. I forgot your shining armor suit was at the cleaners," I sigh, only mostly kidding. I can't hide my disappointment very well.

He arches a brow at me. "Would you rather I leave her—"

"No. No. Of course not," I say. "I'm just being self-ish. I want all of your time and attention."

Leaning over, I move to kiss his cheek, but he turns his head and catches me with his mouth. Stormy takes the hint and scatters off the bed as Ian presses me back onto the pillows, his kisses moving down my neck.

"Oh, I can definitely give you *all* my attention...Let me show you..."

I n the bright light of day, we arrange with Billy to get Mackenzie back to her hotel. Before he arrives, I dig out the front walk from the wall of snow that has accumulated while we hibernated. There are traces of where Billy made his way to the door, but they're already covered back up. It takes longer than anticipated but the solitary exercise at least keeps me from having to face Mackenzie with my lies still fresh on my lips.

Watching as Mackenzie gives Stormy a final ear scratch twists my gut with shame even more. Soon enough our time here, as blissful as it was, will most likely fade into our distant memories.

I should confess before things get too far between us.

But it's already too late for that.

I've dug this hole for myself and every time I think it's the right time to tell her what I've done the words stick stubbornly in my throat.

I've ruined all of this for myself. And for her.

Every kiss is tinged with guilt. Every touch is lined with shame. Every glance is shadowed with regret of how much the truth is going to hurt her. But on the other hand, the thought of my daughters, and my love for them, feels like something I shouldn't be ashamed of. And I'm not ashamed of them at all. On the contrary, I am fucking proud of them. My shame is purely on me for lying about them to Mackenzie.

When Billy arrives to ferry us to the hotel, Mackenzie takes one last look around the cabin. "I don't think I'll ever forget this place." Her eyes land on the gold book on the coffee table and a heated look covers her face as she glances at me from under her lashes. "And I definitely won't forget that book."

Thoughts of places that book directed us to both physically and emotionally flood through me and I can't help but smile back and wrap my arm around her waist. "I'll buy us a copy at the first opportunity."

She reaches up and pulls me into a kiss so gentle and sweet that my chest aches. I'm going to miss this so much. Having her within an arm's length of me has spoiled me. With her leaving it's dawning on me already how alone I'm going to feel.

Like Mackenzie, I'm a loner by nature. I don't need to have somebody with me at all times. And I treasure the serenity of solitude when I get it. But now that I've had her with me, I can see the value of a real partner, someone who you're comfortable with even when quiet.

I never had that with Brianna. Hell, towards the end, I couldn't stand to be in the same country as her. My own wife. I'd given up hope of finding someone like Mackenzie. Someone I could feel like this with. Someone you want to share every moment with feels like a rare gift.

The thought that I have to return that gift stabs me in the gut as Billy calls from the doorway, "If you folks are ready…"

I force a wooden smile. Guilt gnaws relentlessly at my psyche after everything that jolly 'old Saint Billy has done for two strangers. Just add it to the pile. I'm collecting kindling for the funeral pyre that is my honor.

"Ready?" Mackenzie asks turning to leave. Fresh snow reflects the now punishing sunlight, blinding us as we make our way to the snowcat. Mackenzie opts to have an arm around me for assistance rather than her crutches and we make slow progress but eventually clamor on board.

My traitorous heart kicks loudly as I force myself to act like we're simply off on some new adventure together, rather than retreating from a perfect illusion that I manufactured in my head suddenly to buy myself time. Maybe for just a little bit longer, I can pretend that there isn't a huge chasm right in front of us waiting for me to fall into it when the truth is revealed.

The longer this goes on though, the harder it's going to be for both of us. That thought alone kills me. Crushes me.

Annihilates me.

I can only imagine what the truth is going to do to Mackenzie.

AFTER SEEING MACKENZIE SETTLED IN HER ROOM AT THE hotel, I steel myself as I approach Chaos Fuel's row of rooms.

I brace for impact as our production manager Lenny barrels my way, arms flapping.

"There ya are. We gotta sitch. Frankie's flipped his wig and pulled a runner." His old Scottish brogue is thick with emotion.

I sigh, scrubbing both hands down my face dramatically. Why am I not shocked our wet blanket bassist finally cracked dealing with the resident hotheads. So much for a smooth festival.

"Let me guess, Emmett is back to his old self with the stupid pranks?"

Lenny barks out an anxious laugh. "Yeah, Emmett mighta crossed some lines with the drunken hijinks.

But anyway, Frankie's hightailed it back to Nashville. Caught the first flight out. I'm surprised he didn't at least text you. Anyway, we're proper fecked now without a bass player."

My temples already start throbbing double-time doing mental logistics untangling this cock-up. It's been mere hours since my last call and somehow, they've already detonated again.

Fucking lovely.

I'm not in the right headspace for this yet, but I have to force my own personal shit into a box in the corner of my mind so that I can focus on my job. Unfortunately, this is going to make helping Mackenzie with her band even harder.

No, not harder, near impossible.

"Lenny, do me a favor and keep this to yourself for a minute, while I try to think this through and figure out how to solve this." If word gets out that Chaos Fuel is splintering right before their show, they might get pulled from the bill altogether. The last thing I need is for the band freshly under my steward to be labeled in the industry as difficult.

Well, more difficult than they already are.

He arches an eyebrow at me curiously, as he scratches at his graying beard. "What are you thinking?"

My fingers itch as I toy with the idea dancing to the front of my brain. I know the songs. I think I know the set list. What I don't know is if I could step in temporarily for one show. And just as the thought pops into my head, my knuckles in my bad hand ache. Sure, it could be painful, but it would hurt less than all of us losing our jobs.

I'm reminded of Mackenzie's words about responsibility, and how it's not just the band that she worries about, but everyone involved. The crew, the vendors, the label, the fans, there are so many more people relying on this show to go on without a hitch that start to weigh on my heart. I need to make this right somehow and if that means I'm forced out of retirement for one day, I'll have to muddle through it.

"I'm thinking I might need to borrow a bass guitar."

CHAPTER 27

ONE LINE

MACKENZIE

I endure Skyler's fifth apology call before my frustration mounts to unbearable heights. My leg throbs, my mobility is limited, yet the chaos I predicted in my absence mysteriously never manifested. It's almost disappointing.

I scowl, warring with bitterness and relief. When did my boys outgrow my wing so completely? Remy of all people evidently handled crisis control without my micro-managing. Perhaps I should joke he has a budding future as a band manager... he'd get a kick out of that.

You know, if the whole rockstar thing doesn't work out...

Irked for distraction, I dial my touchstone, my calm in any storm - Chelsie, my best friend, untouched by the grease and gears that turn the music industry machinery.

The familiar "Mac Attack!" greeting washes over me before I can even utter a hello. My first genuine smile in what feels like hours spreads, my tension easing just a little bit.

"How's my bedridden badass boss bitch doing?" she demands without preface.

I exhale, the mundane acceptance of my old friend starts thawing my icy doubts. "Oh, you know, the usual, plotting hostile takeovers from my hotel bed...Actually, not bed-ridden, but close enough, I guess."

Her cackle bursts loud enough to echo. "Well, I expect The Killers to be your next target opening act when you roll through Vegas next, given the state of your current prey. Murderous Crows are killing it."

"Consider it done, benevolent dictator," I volley back, practically hearing her beaming from miles away. My usual bite that's been gone for the last couple of days returns, bolstered by her optimistic normality. "Enough about me on the disabled list though, how's my gorgeous godson? And his partner in crime, Lella?"

"Well, they're both in heaven since we're watching Chip for Theo and Bea while they're in Dubai for meetings. That dog has never been so spoiled, or worn out, the poor thing. He thinks he's still a puppy."

The conversation devolves into silly Jett and Lella

anecdotes, and my stress is momentarily muted as I laugh along about their latest antics. I knew I could count on her to distract me.

"...I swear if that dog chews a hole in one more piece of clothing, he'll have to knit us each a whole new wardrobe."

Chelsie's outrage over Chip dissolves into giggles. Soon, Jett and Lella's exploits are thoroughly dissected, and talk meanders, avoiding my snowy misadventures, though it looms ominously.

"You're still coming home for Christmas, right?" she asks, a bit anxious. "These two have special presents for you that they made."

"Ooh, more handmade gifts," I say, thinking about my fridge at home, covered in their artwork. All of them were 'special presents.' "I'm running out of room on my fridge. I'm going to have to start framing things soon."

"Let's just say these are canine-related, so keep your expectations in check."

I can already picture the numerous crayon-colored drawings of Chip that are about to decorate my apartment. "Well, tell them I can't wait to see them."

Finally, she pounces in typical fashion. "Soooo, anyone special keeping your bed warm up there through this ordeal?"

I nearly choke on my tongue. "What? No. I mean, it's been busy handling band drama..." The lie tastes sour, and even my ears hear the unnatural pitch of my voice betraying me.

"Methinks the lady doth protest too much," Chelsie teases. "Spill, woman. Is there a hot medic playing 'Dr. Feelgood' while you recover? An orderly with benefits? What about that guy who rescued you that you texted about? What happened to him?"

I squirm, knowing that trying to evade her is futile once she scents gossip. "It's...not exactly like that. The guy who rescued me, his name's Ian. He's another band manager from the label also here for the festival."

"Oooh, having an intraoffice romance? Scandalous."

I roll my eyes before genuine emotion creeps in. "I don't know Chels...it's complicated, but it's also just so easy with him? I got snowed in with him at his cabin after I was released from the clinic, and we just connected somehow. But..."

Her tone softens. "But it's got you freaking out. I can tell from here."

My throat tightens more. "Am I completely losing it?"

"Oh, sweetie," Her compassion flows warmly through the line. "It's about damn time you lost it a little."

"It's just...I've never felt like this, Chels." I hate the tremor in my voice revealing vulnerability, even with her. "We survived a fucking broken leg and a blizzard together, of course, emotions ran high. But now we're back in the real world and yet I can't shake this, this pull toward him."

I grit my teeth against the threat of tears I'd deny later. Traitorous tears. Tears I *never* let loose. Tears that make zero sense.

She doesn't respond, patiently letting me get it all out.

Damn her.

"Everyone assumes I'm married to my ambitions, which isn't entirely wrong. It's exactly who I've been. That driven meticulous persona is *safe*, it's my armor. You know that about me. I've always been that way. But with Ian, that ice just melts. And I can't rationally explain why. I can't rationalize any of it." Frustration punctures the dam, and I swipe viciously at my wet cheeks. "How can I already be imagining a future with him when logic screams it all just happened because of the situation we were forced into? When did I lose my fucking mind?"

"Oh, honey," Chelsie waits out my ragged breathing. "Maybe you finally found your heart?"

I scoff weakly. "What does that even mean?"

Her smile somehow radiates through the phone. "You gotta stop treating matters of the soul like a freaking spreadsheet, Mac. Stop analyzing and stop running away from vulnerability. Just surrender to this one, it sounds like he might be worth it."

I absently trace patterns on the cheap duvet,

remembering my last intimate encounter with Ian. His whispers. His touch. The phantom of his arms steadies me enough to voice my scariest truth.

"But Chelsie, the fall from feeling this much about someone? So soon? It could ruin me... It already feels too dangerous, and it's only been a few days."

"But, and hear me out, what if there's no fall at all?"

If.

There's that word again. The insipid title of the book that started this whole entire thing.

Betting everything on a two-letter word seems insane. But maybe...

Maybe.

That word at least has five letters.

I find Brad, Emmett, and Stefan of Chaos Fuel out smoking behind the loading dock, no doubt hiding from the fresh hell now erupting with Frankie's speedy departure. Their expectant faces drop as they see my grave expression.

"So, I assume you are all aware that Frankie skipped town?"

A fresh wave of groans and grievances ensue at my confirmation. I let the venting run its course, weathering the rising tension headache.

Emmett crushes his cigarette under a boot. "That fucking asshole had no sense of humor. Couldn't take any jokes without acting all offended and shit."

Stefan shakes his head. "Dude, you shoved snow down his pants in front of everyone. I'd bounce too if you humiliated me like that just for laughs."

"Oh, come off it, we were all mostly drunk during the blackout," Emmett fumes, though guilt flashes across his features before his defiance returns. "And it's not my fault he never wanted to cut loose with us."

Brad sighs, intervening. "Yeah, but that wasn't his first hazing. You were on him all week with other bullshit."

The drummer throws his hands up theatrically. "It's boring messing only with you fuckheads. I swear none of you appreciate quality jokes anymore." Despite attempting to sound indifferent, remorse creeps into his tone.

"Well, too bad you probably can't play bass and take his place instead, since you can't drum for shit either," Stefan grumbles.

"Dude, that's harsh." Emmett seems truly hurt by the jab.

I loudly clear my throat before resentments boil over again. "Look, what's done is done, pointing fingers won't bring him back. Let's talk options going forward."

Emmett kicks out at a nearby snowbank in frustration. "It's not fucking fair! We finally get a huge festival gig, and that flakey jackass ghosts it sideways."

"So, what now?" Stefan asks, uncharacteristically solemn as he takes a long drag of his cigarette. "Does the label bail on us now?"

All eyes turn to me, the newcomer manager expected to work miracles, apparently. I force an assured tone that I don't entirely feel. "Now, we uphold our contract to avoid further complications. I have an idea, but it's...unorthodox."

I hesitate before divulging my nuclear contingency to salvage this trainwreck. No sense delaying the blast though.

"How opposed would you lads be to me filling in on bass for the festival?"

Three voices say in surprised unison, "Whoa..."

I ADJUST THE UNFAMILIAR BASS ACROSS MY SHOULDER, TRYING to shake out sporadic tremors from stale nerve damage as we finish mapping out the setlist. We focus the rehearsals on older Chaos Fuel tracks that use common chord progressions to simplify the transitions. The idea is to minimize any elaborate technical solos to not test fate...or the physical therapy that I definitely ended prematurely all those years ago.

As we launch into *'Bone Crush,'* what starts as lingering stiffness progresses to searing agony by the bridge. I clench my jaw against betraying any visible winces. I'm determined to power through. But as we restart the anthemic *'Devil's Chariot,'* a heaviness settles across my knuckles worse than the ill-fitted guitar. By the second verse, my fingers freeze up, preventing any fretwork whatsoever.

I'm forced to stop playing with a growled curse. Three sets of eyes swing in my direction as our notes die off in a chaotic mess.

"Sorry guys, maybe I'm not up for this after all." I force a weak smile through the waves of pain now coursing up my forearm. So much for smooth sailing on my triumphant return to the stage. Though to be fair, it's probably for the best. I've got enough to deal with.

But now, that leaves us right and truly fucked. All of us.

A tense silence falls over us as the band exchanges uneasy looks, my maimed hand calling our bluff for this harebrained save attempt. I really should have known better. Known my limitations. I can't fucking do everything, even though I want to. Hell, I can't even keep this band together, so maybe I can't do anything at all.

Just as eruptions recommence over our narrowed options, a knock at the door of our practice space interrupts us. We all stiffen seeing Logan, Murderous Crows' renowned bassist, hovering at the threshold holding a six-pack as an awkward peace offering.

"Hey, just wanted to check in on that bass loaner." His amiable tone dies reading the mood. "But uh...seems you guys have bigger issues so I'll just..."

He places the six-pack on a nearby table and moves to duck out when inspiration strikes me dead on.

"No, wait!" I lurch to my feet, struck by possibility. "Your timing's brilliant actually. How do you fancy substituting as a Chaos Fuel honorary member tomorrow? My fret hand is downright fucked, and well, now we all are."

Logan blinks while the rest of the band perks up. They gape open-mouthed as the magnitude of the offer sinks in. But Logan looks like he might be on board. He's curious at least.

"I'd have to ask the guys and Mac, but I don't see why not," he says, rubbing his jaw thoughtfully. "I mean, I know most of your songs. I think."

Brad finds his voice first. "Fucking hell, you'd consider it? That's incredibly decent of you, man."

"We'd be beyond honored," Emmett crows, scrambling up to shake his hand eagerly. "Hell, we all love your stuff."

Amused surprise touches Logan's sharp features before a genuine willingness settles in. "Well shit, I'm happy to help if I can." He turns to me. "We should talk to Mackenzie, and make sure this isn't going to be a problem."

"Right," I nod. "I'll go talk to her."

Fuck. Now I have to admit to something else to her. I'm a shit manager who can't keep his band together.

Mental note to Mackenzie that I'll never mention: Sure, jump into a relationship with me. I'm a lying loser who can't do a fucking thing right. What's not to love?

My mental notebook is getting fucking full.

A knock precedes Ian shuffling into my room, his smile not quite reaching the strain in his eyes. I've already heard the news about the band's bassist skipping town, and his filling in, but he doesn't know that I know. I brace for impact, taking in his worn edges as he sinks onto the bed.

"So, change of plans it seems. My reckless reprobates are suddenly short one bassist for the festival."

He proceeds to explain the lineup adjustment opportunity, but I catch only pieces. I'm distracted tracing the new shadows in his face. The last hours etched deeper grooves of tension around his mouth, faint bruises underscoring his downcast eyes. Marks of someone shouldering simmering troubles he doesn't want to give a name to. I can't help but think about how much stress he's under since taking on this new role.

I tune back in as he finishes explaining the angle to involve Logan in the band's set, a now familiar crease between his brows that betrays the lightness in his tone deepening. I want to wipe it away. Soothe his distress somehow.

"Obviously no pressure in the last-minute loan, but Logan is up for it. Of course, I wanted to discuss this before committing your guy. So, what do you think?" He attempts a roguish grin that my sudden scrutiny cuts short. "Mackenzie?"

I realize my fixation on him as his façade of control shows itself. Something in my chest twinges, and I'm hesitant to pry where I'm not invited, but I'm even more unwilling to ignore his obvious suffering. Obvious to me anyway.

"Ian, are you really okay? And I want the truth this time, no more brush-offs."

His pained gaze drops to his restless hands, thumb worrying his faintly scarred knuckles. When he finally speaks, the admission sounds like it's dragged unwillingly from some deep hollow inside of him.

"I suppose...this debacle with the bassist has rattled my confidence a little bit. Questioning my own competencies and all." He attempts a sardonic chuckle, but it cracks brittle, letting me know how he truly feels. "Maybe I'm not cut out for the hot seat after all. Barely had time to memorize everyone's names before fucking chaos struck. And I clearly failed at damage control if Frankie could fly away faster than I could even know about the problem."

"That's not your fault--"

He shakes his head bitterly, a man unaccustomed to fumbling control suddenly losing it. "Now it feels like they're all looking to me to snap solution after solution like a magician. And I've got nothing but dead doves up these hopeless sleeves." He picks at the rolled-up wrists of his button-down shirt helplessly.

"Well, that's darkly poetic and all, but seriously--"

His eyes find mine again, hints of shame darkening the stormy green before turning away again. "Maybe you should take over primary management here. At least until I get my feet under me." He tries for a self-deprecating smirk, but uncertainty tarnishes this man who I know rarely asks for help. Hell, he's the *fucking hero* in everything I know about him. Behind his troubled eyes, a real fear of inadequacy looms large, but it doesn't feel complete, either. There's something more bothering him, and I'm itching to uncover whatever else is snagging at his spirit. "You know how to do all this. I obviously don't."

My hand covers his gently, my heart aching over the harsh self-judgment he's putting on himself. It's too much. It's way too fucking much.

"Ian, you're being way too hard on yourself. No one expects you to be perfect, least of all me."

His shoulders relax slightly as warmth returns to

those emerald eyes, finally daring to meet mine again. Bolstered by his response, I shift closer, urgent that he understands this. He *has* to know he's better than this.

"Frankie ditching isn't your shortcoming. There's no way that's your fault. Like you said, you haven't even had a chance to find your footing as manager before everything spiraled out of control."

I trace the redness now stretching across his knuckles, the obvious swelling brought on by the sacrifice he made in the name of some kind of duty to the band. He doesn't owe anyone anything. Not a damn thing. Least of all pain.

"Give yourself permission to be human in the role. Trust that your team's got your back too. I've been at this for years and I'm still learning. Plus, you've got a great group of people to lean on. And as for doubts?" I school my features into a stern frown, eliciting another flicker of a smile from him, "I absolutely forbid them in my presence going forward, sir. There's no room for that nonsense. I believe in you."

My final admission escapes low but fervently, surprising even myself. Reluctant hope stirs as I see the tension release its grip on him as he turns my palm up to cradle between both hands, lifting my wrist to his lips.

"What would I do without you?" His whisper brushes my racing pulse, thumbs sweeping distracting circles, lingering before he adds, quieter, "I suppose I should also confess…I did initially try to stand in on the bass."

He flexes his left hand, lip curling.

"Cocky idiocy of me to think these damaged nerves and my atrophied skill somehow qualified me to play like I used to." His expression turns rueful as he massages the faint web of surgical scars. "A few fumbled chords quickly clarified to me what a stupid idea that was. Couldn't even manage the basics before it all seized up. Too little too late trying to force any function back."

"It's admirable as hell you were ready to fill in at a moment's notice yourself to keep things on track. I don't know anyone else that would do that. It was noble of you to even try." One thing I've learned in this business; it's the devils with the smooth skin and the angels who show their scars. I know which one Ian is.

He attempts to shake off the failure, but bitterness creeps back into his tone. "Just added insult to injury all around. At least the guys were kind enough not to mock me, the 'legendary Ian Summer' laid low by a petty twinge."

My chest twists hearing him internalize his struggles so severely. I brace his hand between both of mine, trying to stop his self-recriminations. "The only foolishness was pushing yourself too hard by being selfless for them. They're lucky to have someone so dedicated fighting in their corner. They should be grateful."

Silence hangs heavily between us in the wake of my outburst before Ian clears his throat gruffly. "I'm sorry, I derailed us with my self-pity party. How are things with you? Is everything going to plan on your end?" His eyes flick meaningfully to my cumbersome brace. "How much havoc happened in your absence, if any? From what I've seen, your crew seems remarkably self-sufficient. Skyler was handling the press queue like a pro."

I can't help a small spark of pride hearing that, and I tamp down the simultaneous envy that I didn't get to see their independence blooming firsthand. I've been managing through texts and calls only so far. "Turns out my methodical micromanaging might have finally drilled some skills into them over the years after all."

I attempt to stretch my throbbing leg to a more comfortable position, trying not to wince. "But don't let Cooper catch you suggesting he could walk a straight line unsupervised. I'll never hear the end of it."

Ian carefully helps prop a pillow under my tender leg. Always the caregiver. "Well, I for one am in awe of anyone who can wrangle that many creative personalities without losing their bloody mind."

His praise warms me, thawing any lingering insecurities I have over my fading usefulness being holed up in my room like this. "We do alright together for the most part. Though, it's more like a chaotic family dynamic on even the best of days." I raise a curious brow in his direction. "What about your motley crew, then? Anything else I should warn Logan about when he fills in tomorrow?"

"Oh, geez...where do I start?"

A SHARP KNOCK AT MY HOTEL ROOM DOOR MAKES ME GLANCE up. I'm thinking maybe Ian forgot something but am surprised when I open it to find Logan standing there looking vaguely ill at ease. Our fearless bassist rarely seeks me out for any sort of one-on-one. And from what I now know, he should be practicing with Chaos Fuel to learn their set list.

"Hey stranger, shouldn't you be rocking out somewhere? I hear you've got a new side hustle." I greet him lightly.

Logan shuffles inside, scrubbing a hand through his shaggy brown hair. "Yeah, cool. Okay. I just uh...wanted to check in, I guess? Since you finally emerged from your igloo or whatever." His eyes flick down, seeming to catch on my leg brace for the first time. "Shit, Mac, what happened to you out there?"

My lips twist wryly behind my coffee. "The lift pole won." I sober slightly, seeing concern blaze in Logan's eyes. "Busted fibula. But it's just a hairline fracture. I'll mend alright. Don't worry about it."

He nods, tension easing from his frame as he joins

me at the small table. We sit in surprisingly easy quiet for a moment, the steam of my coffee curling between us.

"It's not the worst injury we've had to power through, huh?" Logan asks eventually, twirling a ring around his finger absently. I furrow my brow, ghosts of the past sweeping in. Of course, he'd mentally revisit the accident that killed Andy and broke his leg. He knows exactly how this feels.

"We survived worse hells," I agree thickly, ignoring the shine of tears in both our eyes. We all somehow made it through to the other side of that valley of shadows together, and we're bonded eternally. And here we are, persevering despite everything thrown in our way.

Logan stands, pulling me gently into a one-armed hug. "We've got this," he vows gruffly. "Let me know if you need anything." I cling fiercer for one breath before stepping back, blinking hard. He seems as though he wants to say something else, but thinks better of it, and clamps his mouth shut.

"Go shine bright with your new rock gods, man." I clap his shoulder once as he turns for the door.

While his visit was out of the ordinary, for him at least, it wasn't unwelcome. I've been thinking a lot about the accident and its aftermath since my own on the slopes. Life is so fragile. Any of us could be stolen any minute without warning. We can be taken completely by surprise to wake up one day and our entire world is upside down.

I do not like surprises.

CHAPTER 30

Welcome to the Chaos

Ian

I gulp the dregs of my third coffee, breath pluming, and scan the bustling grounds. After all of the prolonged delays from the blizzard, the festival's chaotic revival reflects my own. We're all just holding disaster at bay by the skin of our teeth.

My phone blares for the dozenth time with another urgent text and I make a beeline towards the stage, taking in the frazzled crews scrambling to get things ready in time. There's been nothing but fuck up after fuck up all morning, and we're starting to cut it real close to when the venue opens for the festival. It's not giving me the warm fuzzies that this is going to go smoothly.

"Hey! Someone cut power over there before we get fried!" The stage manager bellows from the lighting booth, frantically trying to figure out the malfunction's origin.

I jump in to help yank cords, isolating the issue as Vickie, the backline manager for the local promoter, barrels up to me wheezing. "Serious problems back here too. The backup generator just crapped out on us." Her eyes bulge dramatically. "Half of your speakers just went dark."

"Please tell me we have a backup for the backup?" Though it's not really a question. I can tell already by the look on her face that I won't like the answer.

I swipe both hands down my face, my adrenaline reserves nearly depleted going against this ultimate trial by fire. Of course, the brutal temperatures would corrode parts never designed for the Siberian levels we're having through today's deceptively mild glare.

"Vickie, tell the techs to yank every non-critical component to check circuits for corrosion or cracks," I order, pulling myself together as my mind whirls through backup options. I need to think fast, and some ancient muscle memory kicks back to life from my playing days when things often went wrong. "It might not be the generator. It's still daylight. We can go without the fancy lighting if necessary. I'll check if the other bands' kits have spare amps or power we can borrow in the meantime."

We split to handle damage control when I spot Mackenzie maneuvering slowly nearby, the walkie-talkie chatter blaring similar meltdowns with her stage. Part of me itches to swoop in and solve her crises too, but she's in careful command of her coordinating crews. My jumping in unasked would only undermine her authority.

I refocus on scouting amplifier options, jaw clenched. The best support I can offer is ensuring Chaos Fuel holds up our festival end without being an additional burden to anyone else. If I can somehow wrangle this mounting madness, perhaps the trial by fire will prove to me that I can do this job.

After extensive amp negotiations, I track Mackenzie down again to give status updates. She stands leaning against a stack of crates, radio held up with a frown as she massages her thigh. My breath catches a little seeing the exhaustion starting to pull at her.

"How's it looking over here?" I ask.

She jumps slightly, then flashes a grateful smile when recognizing me. "Oh, from minute to minute I couldn't say for sure. But somehow things are staying tits up just enough to keep things interesting."

"Tits up, huh?" I chuckle, forcing my dirty thoughts at bay. "Don't tell me the language of my homeland is rubbing off on you."

"We can be crude here, too, you know."

I feign an unrecognizable accent, "Oh, it's just so... how do you say in your country...vulgar?"

She lets out an outburst of a laugh, and humor glimmers through the clear strain in her gorgeous eyes. I have to hamper the impulse to wrap protective arms around her, irked to see the pain she's trying to hide beneath the surface. She's hurting, and it kills me.

"What can I do to help?" I nod to where her fingers are attempting to knead the tightened muscles through her brace. "Do you need a hot compress or something to get you through the last mile here? Do you have your pain medicine with you?"

"No. I'm fine, really." Mackenzie attempts to wave off my concern, but her fatigue slips through.

Not liking her struggling alone, I catch her hand, brushing her delicate knuckles. "You know all you have to do is ask, and if I can help in any way, just say the word..."

Her eyes flutter shut briefly, leaning into the support of my palm almost imperceptibly before catching herself. My thumb traces circles on the back of her hand longingly where onlookers can't see. She rallies with a rueful squeeze of my own hand.

"Careful Mr. Summer. Any more chivalry from you and rumors of you and me will spread through this festival like wildfire, if they aren't already." Her smile dimples up at me, erasing her pain momentarily. I trace the faint lines crinkling the corners of her eyes, my pulse stuttering, happily stalled in this oasis between the catastrophes raging around us.

The radio at her hip erupts with fresh demands. I watch her steel spine straighten, the staunch leader facade sliding back into place as she returns to the anarchy. But I also notice, beneath the projections of tireless strength, real exhaustion shadows her now. And I'm afraid what toll this unrelenting pace that she refuses to share will take on her. It can't be good.

My hands flex helplessly as I watch her turn away to respond to the chatter, wanting to offer stability she's too proud to accept from me openly.

My hero status with Mackenzie is over, and I'm not sure how I feel about that.

I shake myself from longing when Vickie jogs up to me again. "Ian, we got bigger fish frying now. Border patrol apparently detained our foreign pyrotechnic artist who never showed up due to problems with their work visa. We need a backup plan."

Tits up is right.

B efore Ian can even fully register the enormity of the fresh disaster, I step forward, gripping his arm. It's my turn to play the hero in this whirlwind of madness.

"As it happens, the pyro crew rigging up the Crows' finale sequence owes me more than a few favors," I say, offering Logan a friendly elbow nudge as he passes by, lugging equipment.

I hold Ian's gaze, refusing to let him get mired in whatever guilt or stubbornness might hold him back from accepting my aid. "I'm sure with some creative coordination, we could arrange some shared fireworks that don't conflict too disastrously across our sets."

I watch a tangle of emotions play across his features. Gratitude wars with pride at accepting my rescue line. He attempts a roguish grin, but obvious weariness dulls his bravado.

"While I appreciate the gesture enormously, borrowing your team's victory lap spectacle feels somehow..." He pauses, searching for diplomacy, "well, tantamount to admitting defeat prematurely, doesn't it?"

His wince gives away that he's clinging foolishly to a lost cause. I soften my voice further, hoping to convey faith rather than pity for what he's going through. I know well how razor-thin that line is that he's walking.

Pride is a bitch.

"Consider it less surrendering than securing reinforcements when you need them. No one doubts Chaos Fuel's abilities, or yours for that matter, if and when this festival finally launches." I risk a comforting hand along his arm. "But even legends need back up against impossible odds sometimes."

The barest spark returns to his gaze at this, something easing behind that formidable facade. I recognize the peace you can find in leaning into someone who intuits your sensitivities, your vulnerabilities, and offers unconditional aid. I recognize it because that was me just days ago with him taking care of me. It wasn't easy to let someone help. Like him, I'm too damn independent.

But sometimes, you just have to give in.

Ian clears his throat gruffly. "Right then. I suppose

it beats sending poor Vicki on an explosives smuggling operation across state lines."

Relief lifts between us, and I can sense a brief but much-needed reprieve before diving back into the relentless tide of the commotion around us.

We just need to get through this show.

What's the old saying? *The show must go on?*

J ust before showtime, I turn to face my cobbled
crew. Logan bounces on his toes itching to slay,
steadfast despite this not even being his real
band. His excitement is infectious, and I love his
enthusiasm. My motley trio is somehow sober today
by some festival miracle, but I'm not looking at the
proverbial gift horse anywhere near the mouth.

"Right mates, eight minutes to show. But I'll skip
the play-by-play, you knuckleheads can't follow
instructions anyhow."

A round of obscene gestures gets laughter flowing,
bleeding nervous tension away. That's more like my
idiots. I soak up the camaraderie before their next
implosion goes off. With these guys, it could happen at
any moment. That's not lost on me. That's *never* lost
on me.

"I'll just say get out there and kick some teeth in, yeah? Like your lives depend on reminding the world who the fuck you are, alright?"

Rowdy cheers shake the thin walls of the trailer we're using as a dressing room. Logan gnashes his pick between sharp teeth. "Hell yes. Let's fucking burn this place down."

I hustle their chaotic energy toward the stage before it combusts backstage first. And before anyone gets the idea in their head to take Logan literally, which I wouldn't put past any of them. It's time for the phoenix to rise for real, or go down in the mother of all flames.

I can feel my chest tighten, preparing to hold my breath the entire set. I won't rest easy until they finish the last note of their last song. And even then, whatever rest comes will be temporary, I'm sure.

I glance left, scanning the bustling wings for a trace of that distinctive splash of violet in the sea of roadies, when a light touch at my elbow redirects me. Mackenzie's trademark smirk tilts playfully.

"Looking for someone?"

I drink her in, chaos settling simply to share space with her again. "Brilliant, was hoping you could sneak a peek. Best seats for scrutiny are right about... here." I gently tug her toward the partition dividing us from thousands of eyes awaiting the band's intro."

I maneuver to spotlight her reaction as the MC finishes the intro and the band takes the stage. For all my snags securing this Hail Mary, nothing compares to Mackenzie's unguarded happiness at this moment. Her lips part in surprise hearing the first tremors of the crowd, raucous and loud despite the chill in the air. To anyone else, I'd chalk her theatrical awe up to showmanship or even mockery. But I recognize the bone-deep relief of hopes rewarded after countless thankless miles paved by her to get here. No critics or cynics can diminish the shine of the hard-won victory sparkling through her gaze. I'm sure my face mirrors hers right now.

Somehow, some way, we've made it work.

At first, I find myself scrutinizing the band with managerial analysis, actively curbing my perfectionist urges to micromanage missed cues or tempo changes. But as their opening song crescendos, raw ability shines undeniably through. The polished veneer that Logan's presence lends admittedly helps, but even without him, Chaos Fuel has *something*. I've always known it. And now, I'm hoping to show it to the world. Surprising pride swells watching my reckless reprobates rising to the occasion, passion earning this chance at redemption.

I'm hopeful, anyway. News about Frankie's quick departure hasn't hit the press yet that I know of. That might all change once it does.

With my reluctant hopes buoyed, I allow myself to soak in the contagious thrill as a fan again right along with the crowd. Logan channels his ultimate showman skills, transfixing even the most jaded in the crowd. And for all their bluster offstage, Chaos Fuel's wizardry at binding some sort of delicate sonic chemistry always struck me. Hearing that familiar spark now through listeners' ears reconnects me to all of the possibilities I first glimpsed when I signed them.

Far too soon their encore erupts into the brilliant, borrowed pyrotechnics, bathing us all in dazzling color. The ovation of the crowd thunders even as the band waves their final goodbyes.

Beside me, Mackenzie turns, eyes shining. "That was amazing." She reaches up to kiss my cheek, her lips warm against my cold skin. "You did it."

"No," I say with a smile that I don't have to force. "We did."

My eyes trace the riot of colors and lilting harmonies onstage before inevitably drifting right, pulled once more into Ian's orbit. His face etched with bittersweet nostalgia and pride for these wayward musicians he has spent countless unsung hours ushering back from the brink of destruction. Only someone like him could have done it. Someone who's been in their shoes.

And though Chaos Fuel's name will flash the largest on tomorrow's headlines and reviews, I don't feel any jealousy at all. They deserve it. *He* deserves it. And the best part is, he won't acknowledge his own part in any of it. He's not a team player, he *leads* the team. I admire that about him. Despite his own vulnerability and fears about his new position, he just gets shit done.

Kind of like me.

The telling muscle twitch of his jaw each time something looks like it might go wrong makes me ache to trace the familiar line and give him kisses until the tightness unknits itself. I have to remind myself that sure, this is a concert, but this is work for both of us. If I let myself, I'd get happily carried away.

My pulse trips on an unexpected epiphany; this ferocious longing's been brewing inside me for far longer than just the time we spent snowed in together. I've been attracted to Ian since we first met years ago. But he was always off-limits in my head.

We were and are work associates, and I always thought that meant nothing could ever happen between us. He was an executive at the label, the hierarchy between us would have been awkward. Plus, I thought he was married, and that's definitely a no-go situation for me.

But now...

Now things are different.

Relationships in this industry are crucial. There's no denying that. It's all barter and trade for favors of one kind or another. But Ian and I are playing on a level field now. We're equals.

Not only are we equals – he respects me, and my experience. Something I am extremely unused to in this business. I've had to forge my way through the male ego bullshit so many times, I've forgotten what actual respect looked like. Usually, when I press an issue that I know is right, anything I get in return is begrudgingly given. Not volunteered.

Ian. Is. Different.

He's selfless. He's loyal to a fault. That was crystal clear in his failed attempt to stand in for Frankie. I could tell right away that it cost him his pride to admit he couldn't do it. But he *did* admit it. He was honest about it and didn't force the issue with some machismo bravado, only to screw everything up in the end. He knew his limits. But he tried. He selflessly tried to fix it himself.

I love that.

And he didn't balk at my offer of help. He understood he needed it and accepted it. Sure, I could see the little dents it made in his pride, but he understood the assignment. He gets that at a festival like this, one band's success is everyone's success. We're all links in a chain here, and if one breaks, we all fall apart.

I think we might make a good team, Ian and me.

We haven't broached the subject, but I think it might be on the horizon for us. I can totally see us working out, doing our own thing, but the same thing at the same time.

I haven't considered a long-term relationship with anyone for a very, very long time. I've been too focused on my career. But looking at him now, and the complex planes that make up his heroic soul make me yearn for that with him.

Growing older with someone always meant

slowing down in my mind, giving up somehow. Not necessarily being 'tied down,' but restricted in some way. I don't feel that at all with Ian. With him, I feel safe, comforted, and allowed to be vulnerable. Basically, all the things I've never felt before.

It's scary as shit, but exciting at the same time.

Fucking hell. Am I really falling for this guy?

He rescues broken damsels in distress on ski slopes, and orphaned kittens buried in snow. Hell, he even rescued Chaos Fuel when they needed it. He reads fast like a motherfucker and can make the best hot chocolate I've ever had from freaking scratch. He chases bad dreams away, and always, *always*, is concerned for my welfare before his own.

He's a fucking unicorn.

Somewhere between whiteouts and blackouts, I fell for this guy. This man who doesn't dim himself during storms, or hide, but shines brighter when he fights them. I'd be happy to warm myself near his flame, anytime.

Who even knew someone like him existed?

Not me.

Color me surprised as fuck.

STILL RIDING HIGH ON CHAOS FUEL'S EPIC SET, SUDDENLY all our monitors cut out minutes before Murderous

Crows are set to headline. Fresh panic erupts over potential electrical issues or damaged cables. Every tech on deck dives into frenetic troubleshooting trying to resolve the video kill before call time.

Amidst the mess I can feel Ian smoothly join the rescue effort, alert to the crisis and already figuring out the shortest path to a resolution. He doesn't announce his intentions loudly to everyone, or make a show seeking praise, he just intuitively tackles locating the damaged inputs and coordinates quick hot swaps. Within minutes of his subtle actions, the monitors flicker promisingly back to life and my monitor crew sighs with relief.

So do I. Once again, my hero saved the day.

What was I saying about unicorns?

I sneak a grateful smile Ian's way as he continues calmly directing stagehands around. And my heart swells realizing that Ian could be a true partner, rising to share burdens wordlessly because my trials are his too.

I need to be careful. I'm getting carried away with all of this Ian worship. My rose-colored glasses are fusing to my face at this point.

As final audio checks commence flawlessly, thanks to Ian's steady troubleshooting, he sidles up to me, smiling. I can see the adrenaline still coursing through him from pulling another victory from near disaster yet again today.

"Sorry to swoop in on your operation uninvited.

Force of habit, leaping to lend a hand..." He presses his palms together apologetically even as satisfaction glints behind his bashful green eyes.

I lay my hand against his wrist, catching his gaze directly. "Don't you dare apologize. You likely salvaged the whole set just by intuitively figuring out the problem. It was..." I fumble for words to convey my sudden swell of emotions. I really am losing it. "Well, I've never had someone dive into my professional mess without asking just because they knew it impacted me too."

His eyes gentle, seeing through to the heart of my awe. How deeply being in sync with someone else strikes a rusty cord after years and years of striving solo against storms nobody else even registered.

Part of my natural defenses whispers, *'danger,'* at giving up any autonomy so willingly to someone suddenly attuned to my inner burdens and needs. But the rest of me pushes that caution to the side, realizing the relief that not weathering every storm alone doesn't mean weakness, it just means that a partnership makes everything easier to face.

What a revelation to have in the middle of a show.

Good god. I'm in so much fucking trouble with this guy.

The riotous spectacle of Murderous Crows' theatrics reaches a fever pitch right in time with my own spiraling emotions. It's no surprise Mackenzie's team has refined showmanship to a science. They clearly learned from the consummate pro beside me, maneuvering every behind-the-scenes twist without breaking a sweat.

Seeing her in her element stirs that now familiar swell of fierce affection. But it also signals the possible ending of our time together.

I don't want it to end.

As the surrounding music rages, uncertainty starts to ache in my heart. Does the end of the show mean the end of us? We never talked about the future, let alone just tomorrow.

Dread creeps in as I imagine our paths diverging

come daybreak tomorrow. Is our going back to the real world going to shatter this fragile snow globe we've found each other in? Is what we have together sustainable in our day-to-day lives?

Or are we beyond that? Could what we've gone through together these last few days be enough to forge a true relationship? Do I even want that?

Of course, I do. With Mackenzie, I absolutely do.

But how do I do that when she doesn't know everything? She knows me like nobody in my life has known me, but at the same time, she doesn't know me at all.

She doesn't know that I'm a fucking selfish coward. My lie of omission is always on the tip of my tongue, wanting to be set free. To hell with the repercussions. But something holds it in, keeps it back, and silences me.

Fear.

My fear of losing her is stronger than anything I've ever felt before. Is that what true love is? Desperately holding on to something you know deep down in your soul you don't deserve?

I watch Mackenzie cheer her band of brothers on through their finale, her stunning face joyfully aglow in crimson and sapphire from the salvaged fireworks show. I'm hit with sudden wretched clarity that losing even a fleeting chance at earning a permanent place in her heart would devastate me.

Ruin me.

But fuck what I deserve. She deserves better.

Better than me.

Who the fuck am I? I'm just a washed-up and broken rockstar with a family she'd never want.

I know I've already doomed us.

Being torn is a real thing. Heartbreak is a fucking physical torment in my chest. I can feel the scars already forming on my heart. But that's the good thing about scar tissue; it's thicker, stronger, and impermeable to pain.

After the deafening final encore, I help Mackenzie carefully navigate the backstage chaos to her hotel before taking my own lonely trek through town to my cabin, back to Stormy, who's been left alone all day.

Festival after parties certainly sound attractive, especially with Mackenzie in attendance, but strangely I crave isolation now. My gut churns with all the suppressed truths that would absolutely condemn me in her beautiful violet eyes.

Outside her hotel, sadness creeps in, chilling me more than the frigid icy air as our impending separation looms large in my mind and heart. Mackenzie pauses before entering, watching ephemeral snowflakes drift under the nearby amber streetlights.

"I almost wish the storm would come back if it meant we could steal a few more of these rare moments alone together." Uncharacteristic hesitation clouds her smile as she timidly turns my way. My fingers tremble, barely containing the urge to pull her close, promising a safety neither of us controls anymore.

I sway forward, my pulse raging arguments to both my heart and my head. Neither one is winning. But the door swings open abruptly as someone leaves the hotel, ruining the enchantment echoing between us.

"Go. Enjoy the party," I say, chastely kissing her forehead. Her scent permeates my senses, and I nearly break and give in. Somehow, I'm able to resist and step back.

"I'll call you first thing in the morning?" she asks, and the hope in her eyes is absolutely devastating.

I'm nearly rendered speechless, but somehow find my voice.

"Of course," I nod noncommittally, and give her a slight bow as I force myself to turn away.

Shoving my hands deeper into my coat pockets, I decide to take a roundabout path through the snow-covered town to my cabin, passing concert revelers still high on emotion from the show on the long walk. Snippets of Chaos Fuel's lyrics hit my ears, sung out of tune, and laced with liquor. Instead of feeling pride for a show pulled off against all odds, all I feel is empty.

All I've accomplished is a set up for failure.

Just fucking tell her.

Nursing the warming whiskey in my frozen fingers, I let the laughs and antics of the guys wash over me as they pass the platinum record I presented after the show back and forth to each other for photos. The typical manic post-festival relief mingles with a surprising sadness knowing the regular grind resumes tomorrow. Even with Christmas right around the corner, work never ends.

My gaze drifts toward the exit, hoping against hope that Ian will change his mind and come join us. I wonder how Stormy survived the day alone. Maybe she tore the cabin to pieces in our absence. Kind of how my heart feels right now.

All of this celebration around me, and I'd rather be there.

The disappointment running through me that we're not going to spend our last night here together is getting overwhelming. I thought for sure we'd been connecting on a deeper level. Something was happening between us. Maybe I was wrong?

"Soooo, rumor has it a certain Brit rockstar-turned-exec-turned-manager was quite the Florence Nightingale caretaker playing to your snowbound damsel in distress. Any truth in it?"

Remy's suggestive smirk cuts through my internal thoughts and I do my best to hide my blush in my glass as the guys chuckle at his not-so-subtle fishing expedition.

I wish I knew how to answer. I wish I knew what to say, what was really happening between us, because all of a sudden, I don't know. I thought I did...

"You guys know my love life isn't a topic of conversation." I fall back onto my old set of group rules. They can talk to me about their relationships all they want, but they can't ask me about mine. It's an unwritten rule, but we all know it's there. I really don't care if it's fair or not.

"C'mon Mac, don't hold out on us," Logan goads, elbowing Remy conspiratorially. "I've seen enough romantic comedies to spot the 'snowed-in' romance trope from a mile away. Plus, I've seen how you two look at each other. Something's happening."

"What's between myself and Mr Summer, if

anything, shall remain classified intel, gentlemen," I hold firm.

They exchange dramatic sighs over my verbal barricades. "You can't blame our curiosity though," Jake pipes up, nudging me shoulder to shoulder. "Who would be so bold as to date Mackenzie Roberts: the Rock Band Dragoness?"

I swat his shoulder playfully, laughing despite myself. Should I confess to just how readily my dragon scales fell away for Ian? With how we recently parted outside the hotel, I'm not so sure.

But more longing looks toward the exit betray my internal war, provoking secret smiles between all of them. I'm not going to be able to shake off any assumptions they're going to make, so I simply shake my head, hiding flushed cheeks behind my glass once more.

I glance down at Logan's now-ringed finger, then over to Skyler, chatting animatedly with a visiting friend and the other band fiancées in the corner. I just discovered five minutes ago that they got married. "Who are you to talk, Mr. Suddenly Married Man? I'm offended I wasn't invited to the wedding, whenever and wherever it was. How the hell did you fit it in when everyone was snowbound?"

His chest puffs a bit as he looks at his shiny new ring, wiggling his fingers, but his smile is rueful. "We got the license in LA before the trip here. We were gonna just have a simple Justice of the Peace thing after New Years. But the bartender in the hotel bar said he was ordained to do weddings when we told him about our plans. And well, one drink led to another, and here we are. Married."

"You might want to double-check those credentials," I say, and catch Skyler looking over at Logan, recognizing the emotion on her face. I wonder if I look like that when I'm looking at Ian.

"We did. We did. And don't worry, I recorded it, Mac," Cooper says pulling out his phone. "Here, check it out."

Watching the makeshift wedding in the hotel bar on the shaky video pulls at something inside me. Skyler's bouquet of bar straws and paper napkin roses is somehow oddly perfect for her. Like me, she's no frills, no fuss. I don't think she even has any makeup on.

Logan looks nervous as fuck, but just as happy. Like he's about to dive into the deepest water he's ever seen. But it's one of those situations where he's learning to swim, not just learning not to drown. There's a difference, and I can see it in him. He took the plunge with confidence.

It feels almost like my kids are growing up. And this one did it without me. I'm not sure how I feel about that.

Obviously, I'm happy for both of them. They are so good together it's almost sickening. All of them are with their respective partners. But there's a twinge in my heart, too, not knowing if I'll ever get to experience that permanence with someone else. I can already feel Ian slipping away from me for no reason.

When the video ends with everyone cheering the 'kiss the bride' moment, I hand the phone back to Cooper, swallowing the hard lump in my throat. "That's amazing. Really. Congratulations, Logan. I'm so happy for you guys."

Everyone eventually heads off to be with their partners; Logan to Skyler, Jake to Cassidy, Cooper to Sloane, and Remy to Monroe. Everyone made the trip today despite the weather just to be here for the special event. They made the effort. And looking at all of their happy faces makes me happy too.

There was a time when Andy died, that I didn't think this would be possible. Things looked so bleak, and our troubles seemed insurmountable for a long time. I never expected this success. I hoped for it. I worked hard for it. But I've never been one to believe that dreams came true.

This one did.

But the thing is, in making this dream happen for all of us, I ignored my own personal dreams. Well, those outside of my career, anyway. It's not that I never wanted a partner, I just never thought it could work. That is, until I met Ian. For some reason, he makes me think a real partnership is possible.

And damn it, I *do* want my own dream to come true.

CHAPTER 36

GUIDING LIGHT

IAN

S tormy blinks slowly, passing silent judgment as I pace grooves into the antique Turkish rugs covering the cabin's wood floors. Even the cat knows I'm a bloody coward avoiding the reckoning that coming clean with Mackenzie would bring.

After days of evading the truth, how can I beg Mackenzie to hear out such shame-faced omissions without torching the fragile connection between us? Is it really as fragile as I think it is?

You forfeited any right you might have had to mercy hiding your bloody kids like criminal sins rather than tell her about them from the start.

Fucking, fucking, fucking coward.

"Fine. You win. I'm going," I mutter to the cat as I grab my coat and the keys to my rental car, self-disgust propelling me back toward whatever uncertain fate awaits me. Now that the roads are all clear, and I've unburied the car from all of the snow it was hiding beneath, it's high time I face the firing squad or lose her anyway once this brief oasis completely dissipates. My brain runs through all plausible narratives, and excuses unfurl wildly as I get to her hotel floor.

The words will come to me. They have to. It was an honest mistake to keep this from her. My wires crossed, and the timing never felt right afterward. And then...I just...I just...*nothing*.

Not a gods damned thing is coming to mind that will fix this.

All I have to do is start, right? And the rest will come to me. If this is real, it will come to me, and everything will be fine.

I raise a shaky hand to knock softly on the door, a small part of me hoping she's fast asleep and dreaming of better things than what I'm about to detonate in front of her.

The handle turns.

Here we go.

Her incandescent smile when she opens the door scatters all coherency straight away. And when she pulls me into a mind-melting kiss without a word, the whiskey she's had is sweet on my tongue and goes straight to my own head. My galloping heart traitorously whispers, *it can all wait until the morning...*

I trace fleeting snowflakes instead of looking Ian in the eyes as we wait outside the hotel for my ride to the airport. It's still dark out since it's so early, but something is off between us this morning, and I can't for the life of me figure out what it is.

Last night was amazing. We barely said a word to each other, just expressing ourselves with our bodies, our hands, our kisses. Our touches said more than I think words ever could. And in that regard, I loved what he had to say. The way that he seems to worship me when we're together, the reverence, is other-worldly. Which in turn, makes me want to do the same for him.

It's so intimate, it's scary.

All of this moment is scary.

"Text me when you land or get home safe," he says,

eyeing the car pulling into the lot warily, and pulling me into a hug. "Both, actually. Text me both."

I bury my face into his neck, my breath pluming in the frigid air around us like a cloud.

"I can't believe you're driving all the way back to LA, just to take Stormy with you," I say, still disbelieving. But then, of course, he is. He just forgets he's supposed to wear a cape to identify him as the hero he is.

"It's only a fourteen-hour drive, give or take," he says with a soft laugh. "You didn't think I'd actually leave her here, did you?"

"Well, no, of course not. But fourteen hours... You sure you don't want me to come with you?" I can feel the barest of his tensing muscles as I ask the question yet again. "I really wouldn't mind."

"No, no. We'll be fine," he says, pulling away and grabbing my suitcase to roll to the waiting car. "Besides, you have another flight home to Vegas for the holiday later this evening to prepare for. Don't worry about us."

I follow him carefully on my crutches to the car, reluctant for the oncoming goodbye. I really don't want to leave him.

"Well, you keep me posted on your journey," I say, wrapping him in a final hug. "Don't forget, I'm invested in Stormy's welfare too. She and I bonded, you know."

"Oh, I'm well aware," he smiles, but his eyes are

still guarded. Those emerald depths are murky now with emotion I can't place. Maybe he's as sad for us to part as I am. Maybe he's just feeling the same way I do and can't find a way to express it.

Maybe. Maybe. Maybe.

"Ok, well, I guess we'll talk soon then," I say, reaching up to kiss him one more time.

What I think is going to be a brief peck goodbye turns into something much more when Ian pulls me close against him, holding on so furiously that I think he might crush me in his strong arms. The kiss becomes desperate, and I give in to the emotions flowing through me, wanting him to know I'm feeling the same. I don't want this to end. Any of this.

He pulls away suddenly, as if remembering himself and where we are, his cheeks flushed red, and not from the cold.

"Sorry," he mutters, his lowered eyes apologetic. "I got carried away...have a...safe flight, Mackenzie."

"Ian..."

I barely get his name out before he's trotting across the parking lot to his car. Goodbyes are hard for everyone, but I had no idea he would be this way about it. Maybe stuff like this is too much for him.

Again – maybe, maybe, maybe.

I'm going to drive myself mad with this shit.

No good choices are in front of me, so I get in the cab, keeping an eye on Ian as we pull away. He glances back over his shoulder at me, but only briefly. He doesn't see me wave goodbye.

The knot in my stomach that started at the end of the festival yesterday tightens. I don't like this feeling.

I don't like it at all.

F ourteen hours. Fourteen long hours on the road with a very ornery cat who doesn't appreciate tight spaces.

I crack the window of my rental car, letting in a blast of cold mountain air. Stormy meows in protest from her cat carrier in the passenger seat.

"Sorry, love," I say, adjusting the heat. "It was getting a bit stuffy in here."

I glance over at the orphaned black cat Mackenzie and I rescued during our idyllic days snowed in together. My heart twists thinking of the incredible woman who now consumes my thoughts. Things escalated so quickly between us, it felt like a dream, but now reality has set back in.

Fucking reality.

As the car descends from the mountains, I dread

the long drive ahead to LA. Nothing but time and the company of a cat, trapped alone with my thoughts, when all I can think about is the secret I still keep. It's never-ending.

Guilt gnaws at me. I should have told her right away, but the more time we spent cocooned in that cabin, falling for each other, the harder it became. I know Mackenzie has written off motherhood for herself. What if she writes me off too once she knows?

It's not exactly something I can keep from her forever, now, is it?

I grip the steering wheel tighter. Mackenzie sees me as some kind of fucking hero after I rescued her from the slopes, and solved problems for our bands during the chaotic festival. I did what any decent human being would have done, and then I was just doing my job.

If only she knew what a fraud I actually am.

She'll know. She'll eventually know. There's absolutely no escaping it, and I'm making it worse every day I don't tell her.

Stormy lets out a plaintive meow, jolting me from my brooding. "We've still got a long ride ahead, little one," I tell her, reaching over to stroke her soft fur through the bars of her crate on the passenger seat. At least I have one female in my life who doesn't make me feel like a complete bastard.

Yet.

The miles of highway unwind before me as I resign

myself to the drive. I plug my phone into the car's stereo system to listen to a stream from the festival show. I need to get lost for a while in my head, and taking mental notes of Chaos Fuel's set is at least one way to do that. The opening chords of "Playing with Fire" pour in. Brad's gritty vocals fill the space around me, transporting me back to the energy of the festival stage. But also to standing side-by-side with Mackenzie, her face bathed in colorful stage lights, head nodding along with the driving bass line. Then I'm overwhelmed with our time together last night... I snap the music off with an impatient stab of my finger.

Bloody hell. What idiot thought that reminder was a good idea? Oh yeah, this idiot.

After hours of listening to one boring podcast after another, I pull off the highway outside Barstow, California, in need of gas and to stretch my aching limbs. As I top up the rental's tank, Stormy meows piteously from her carrier.

"I know it's confining, sweetheart," I say, "but it's safer for you there. We only have a couple more hours to go. Sit tight." This newly rescued cat is still somewhat unfamiliar with me. I wish I could let her wander freely, but I don't dare on such a long drive. We've come this far without incident, I don't want to push our luck. I pour a splash of water into her collapsible travel bowl, and she laps it up eagerly. At least I can do something right at the moment.

I stretch my stiff limbs and take in lungfuls of

sharp desert air. The setting sun streaks the sky indigo and pink behind two young girls chasing one another nearby. The older one can't be more than seven. Her hair, more golden than Hayley's cornsilk blonde, bounces behind her as she dashes around her younger sister. My chest tightens, missing my girls, and anxious to see them.

Still, the scene is so reminiscent of them; their giggles, the way the little one's nose crinkles when she smiles, that a lump forms in my throat.

"Daddy, come push me!" the younger girl pleads, clambering up onto a swing.

Her father chuckles, abandoning his conversation with who I assume is the girls' mum to stride over. "Alright, Daisy, hold on tight now."

As he gives her a push, a memory flashes through my mind of pushing Hayley and June on the swings at our neighborhood park back when we were all still together. I'd give anything to return to those simpler days. But really, nothing is ever simple. If I'm really honest with myself, it wasn't simple then, either.

Part of me leaped at the extra time with them for Christmas, especially now, when I'm questioning so much about my relationships and what future I envision for my family. But the other part of me feels another wave of turmoil crashing over the roiling sea inside. That revelation for Mackenzie, whenever it comes, coupled with my growing feelings for her.... It could change everything.

It *will* change everything. And if I'm right, it will ruin everything.

As I turn away, melancholy creeps over me at the thought of my own daughters' smiles awaiting me in England. My secrets. I rake a hand through my hair, heaving a sigh.

"One dilemma at a time, mate," I mutter to myself. For now, it's back on the long, lonely highway ahead. It's only about a hundred more miles home, but the miles between problems never seem quite far enough.

CHAPTER 39

DON'T DELETE THE KISSES

MACKENZIE

I scroll through my text conversation with Ian for the hundredth time, chewing on my bottom lip. His last response to me telling him I landed safely still glares up at me, mocking in its brevity.

IAN: Good.

One word. The digital equivalent of a door slamming in my face after the connection we made over those intimate days snowed in. I know the bubble had to pop and real-life rush back in, but I wasn't ready for...*this*. Distance with radio silence topping it. Question marks where intimacy once flared brightly.

Maybe I'm reading too much into a single text. Ian did have that long-ass drive ahead of him after all. And here I sit waiting for my flight to Vegas, while he's probably hundreds of miles away by now. Kinda wild how close we seemed just days ago, compared to feeling worlds apart now.

I absently twist my porcelain and gold ring, yet another one of the nervous habits I've had since I was a kid. Its delicate flower design and gold band was a gift from my mom when I started managing Murderous Crows after high school.

I sometimes wonder what she'd make of the hardened, cynical woman I've become, married more to my career than any regular guy. Until maybe Ian. Somehow, in seeing the gentle care he showed Stormy, and how I fell right in with that care, I caught a glimpse of a nurturing side in myself I scarcely knew existed.

But does Ian see that potential lasting future for us that I'm suddenly scared to lose? I stare once more at that icy one-word text, feeling my heart squeeze.

Maybe the fantasy really did die along with the last glowing embers in the fireplace back at that cabin. Maybe now in the ashes, it's time for some hard truths.

Chelsie will know what to do about all this.

I hope.

I'M ATTACKED BY TWO PINT-SIZED MISSILES THE MOMENT I'M through Chelsie's front door.

"Auntie Mac!" her kids cry in unison, barreling into me. I can't help but laugh even as I stumble backward a little under the force of their hugs, bracing myself carefully to keep weight off my injured leg.

"Gentle with your auntie right now," Chelsie reminds them from the kitchen. "She's still getting better from her skiing ouchie."

Jett's eyes go wide. "Sorry!" He reaches to gently hug just my waist instead while Lella asks if I want to sit down and play with the dog.

"I'm alright, munchkins." I ruffle both their hair affectionately, limping further inside. "Nothing can keep me down too long. And where is this dog you're so excited about?"

My best friend emerges, dish towel flung over one shoulder. "They haven't left this poor dog alone since Theo dropped Chip off," Chelsie says, shaking her head with a wry smile. As if on cue, I hear the scrabble of paws on tile and turn to see a spotted mutt bounding toward me, tongue lolling.

"We drew pictures of him for you," Jett informs me proudly, and loudly. He's never had a volume button. He grabs his younger sister's hand, both of them bouncing excitedly. "Can we give Auntie Mac her Christmas presents now, Mom? Pleeeease?"

Chelsie rolls her eyes. "They've been begging me all day. I finally had to cave just to get some peace."

She winks at me. "I figured one early Christmas gift wouldn't hurt."

The kids race off to retrieve their drawings and I follow Chelsie into the kitchen, a meandering Chip following patiently behind. I idly scratch his ears as she pours us glasses of wine.

"So..." Her leading tone immediately sets me on alert for questions about Ian. "How's your man holding up after playing nurse?"

"He's..." I trail off, staring at my brace with a small shake of my head. With the distance between us, I'm no longer certain how to describe this thing with Ian. But before Chelsie can inquire further, the kids rush back in to distract us with their drawings. My sigh of relief makes Chelsie snort. We clink our wine glasses silently; a toast to conversations merely postponed. Interrogations will keep for later.

After a long evening of playing with the kids, I sink onto the couch beside Chelsie, gratefully elevating my injured leg onto the ottoman. The kids are tucked happily in bed, their excitement and rough housing with Chip finally giving way to yawns. Chelsie's husband Noah is off tinkering in their huge garage full of classic cars, giving us girls alone time to chat.

In their wake, a heavy silence hangs between my best friend and me. She wordlessly tops off our wine glasses. Liquid courage for the conversation she's been biding her time for all evening.

I take a large gulp before meeting Chelsie's probing gaze. "Alright, go ahead. Ask me anything."

Chelsie leans forward, eyes glittering with curiosity. "Spill it, hon. What happened with Ian after you two emerged from that sexy little snowed-in cabin?"

I twist my ring absently. "I don't know Chels...we didn't make any big declarations or labels before leaving Aspen. But the connection felt so..." I trail off, searching for the right word.

"Real?" Chelsie supplies gently.

I nod, confusion and hurt welling up. "But now back in the real world, he's barely spoken to me. Just stupid one-word texts."

Chelsie grabs my hand, ceasing my nervous spinning. "Have you told Ian how it makes you feel when he goes silent like this?"

"Well, no," I admit. "What if he doesn't feel the same way as me? If this was just a fleeting thing for him?"

She's patiently silent, letting me sort my jumbled thoughts.

"I just don't get it," I sigh, taking a large swig of merlot. "Ian and I have known each other for years professionally. But during the festival was the first time we ever really talked, you know? And I felt this intense connection between us."

Chelsie nods sagely. "So, what was stopping you two from exploring things before the little Winter Wonderland lockdown?"

I snort. "For starters, Ian was married. Off-limits. And I honestly didn't think he even saw me that way." I shake my head with a wry laugh. "I figured I was doomed to be wed solely to my career, with a gaggle of rowdy rockstars as my eternal children. But now they're all pairing off..."

"Things change," Chelsie says softly, instinctively topping off our glasses again. She sure knows how to loosen me up. "That spark was clearly already there; it just needed the right ignition." She studies me intently. "The better question is, now that you've had this taste of something deeper with Ian, do you want more?"

I fall silent, staring into my wine. Do I? "Before the isolation of the cabin, I'd never dreamed of anything beyond the transient flings and adrenaline-fueled world I live in. But Ian makes me imagine something different...quiet mornings wrapped in each other's arms...a true partner to share this crazy life with...maybe even..."

"A family?" Chelsie asks gently.

I release a shaky breath. "I don't know if that's meant for someone like me. If Ian even sees me as potential mother material. Lord knows *I* never have before now." I swallow hard against the ache building in my throat. "But maybe? Someday?"

Chelsie takes my hands in hers. "You'll never know unless you talk about it with him."

"Yeah, but when? All I'm getting is a near brush-off

now, and he's headed to England for two weeks. Not exactly the best time."

"Oh, honey." Chelsie squeezes onto the loveseat beside me and pulls me into a hug. "This is important. Find the time to lay it on the line. Life's too damn short —especially in your crazy rock n' roll world. When Ian's back from England, surprise him by being the bold woman I know you are. Worst case, you get closure." She winks conspiratorially. "Get him something for Christmas and deliver it to him in person once he's back. Nothing major or 'relationship labeling.' You know, just something small and thoughtful."

Despite my doubts, I feel myself smiling slightly in response, knowing exactly what to get him. And maybe she's right...maybe it is time to make a stand to find out if this unexpected connection with Ian is already fading, or if the attraction between us just needs re-sparking.

I down the last of my wine in one long swallow. As much as my talk with Chelsie has centered me, chilled uncertainty still gnaws at the edges of my buzz. I'm used to always being the one in control when it comes to romantic chemistry. But this time feels different. Rawer.

Maybe I'm the lone lit match in this scenario. My next move with Ian will determine if the combustible heat between us blazes back to life...or fizzles straight back out to cold, hard ashes.

"Refill?" Chelsie interrupts my silent thoughts and

grabs the wine bottle. I nod gratefully, the rich aroma settling my crazy emotions temporarily. *I'm glad I stopped with the pain pills with all of this wine...geez.*

Chelsie's scanning her phone as she settles back beside me on the couch when her motions still, brows knitting. "Hey, you remember that merch girl who bailed on you guys ages ago? The one causing all the press drama?"

I tense involuntarily. No one from the band has breathed her name in a long while, yet it never strays far from my thoughts. "Nyx," I reply shortly, pulse already quickening. Just the sound of her name out loud makes me cringe inwardly. "What about her? Whose life is she trying to ruin now?"

Chelsie turns her screen so I can view the brief obituary she pulled up. The photo steals my breath – it's our old merchandise vendor, who then went on to make our lives a living hell. Nyx's sly smirk is captured eternally in the tiny pixels of a picture I've never seen of her before. It's her for sure, though the mischief in her eyes that was always there has dulled. *'Unexpected passing,'* the brief death notice cryptically states. But I know all too well the demons who likely overtook that chaotic soul in a final lethal dose.

"Jesus," I whisper, chest constricting. I picture the turmoil and lies she wove and then tried to blackmail us with. Yet there were also probably desperate moments when I might have reached out more as a mentor. *If* I'd seen them. I never saw them. All I saw in her was what she wanted to show. And all of it was a lie. In the end, she couldn't be trusted.

In the end...

Chelsie grips my shoulder, centering me back from spiraling regret. The past can't be changed.

I lift my glass in a silent toast regardless of my opinion of her. She had demons, for sure. And she introduced everyone else to them, including the tabloid world, causing us nothing but headaches. But any life lost is a loss of potential. She certainly squandered hers.

I find the article on my own cell and send it to the Murderous Crows group chat. Then I turn my phone off. I don't want to see the cheers and celebrations of her death. Deserved or not, that's not up to us to decide.

And I don't want to think about endings right now.

J etlag drags at me as I shuffle through the Heathrow terminal, and once outside, the damp London air bites after California's constant sunshine. I sling my rucksack higher and head for the taxi queue, ready to crash at my hotel. I'm used to traveling and being on the road, but these last few journeys have been hard, even for me.

Stormy is settled in her new surroundings and under the very capable watch of my neighbor's exuberant children. They'll look in on her daily and keep me posted on any hiccups. The cat seems to be more well-adjusted to the change than I am. Fair play.

I opted for a hotel rather than staying with Mum. Our relationship strains a little more each visit home. Her image for my life here collides harder all the time with the reality I've built for myself in LA. But she still expects me and the girls for the full Boxing Day experience in a few days. It'll be torture for me, but I can't find it within myself to deprive them.

As I wait in the cab line, I pull out my mobile to text Brianna that her daughter's wayward father has landed safely. My screen mocks me with my last sent message to Mackenzie.

ME: Good.

One bloody word after all our time together in that cabin, falling into each other. Into possibilities that still confound me, especially alongside raising two little girls.

I shove the phone back in my pocket, guilt churning my empty stomach. What I said to Mackenzie, or what I haven't said, feels equivalent to locking her out in the cold after the connection we forged. She deserves more than bloody silence. But how do I bridge this widening ravine between us without sending her bolting for good?

Before I spiral further, my taxi pulls up. Time for a shower at the hotel to revitalize, then off to Brianna's to scoop up my daughters into a joy already clouded by half-truths. My world here clashes even more with the new fragility taking root across the ocean. But I can only triage one earthquake at a time.

I can't help but chuckle to myself, *'See Mackenzie? I'm no fucking hero.'*

I RENT A CAR FOR MY STAY, AND PULL UP OUTSIDE THE HOUSE from my previous life when a "forever" with Brianna seemed plausible. The front garden's tacky holiday display assaults my bleary eyes. It must be her new boyfriend, Axel's work. The latest temporary distraction she's trotting off to Tenerife with rather than spend Christmas with her own children.

My scarred knuckles whiten reflexively on the steering wheel as I put the car in park. I know Brianna's not evil, but "Mother of the Year" isn't in the cards for her either. We were doomed years ago when my injury ended my playing career, and with it, the flashy lifestyle Brianna felt entitled to. It looks like she's still keeping up appearances, gaudy as it is.

I smooth my features as June and Hayley burst out the front door. Their little limbs pummel me with ecstatic hugs. "Daddy!" Laughing, I scoop them both up, breathing in their sweetness and pushing away the bitterness that was creeping into my mood.

Over their little shoulders, I pass over Brianna's impassively polite gaze and land on her new boy toy. Axel eyes my faded punk shirt with clear disdain.

I looked him up when Brianna first mentioned him, making sure my girls were in somewhat decent company so far away, and discovered he's in a boy band. I guess there's no accounting for taste, but the fade haircut he's sporting isn't doing him any favors.

No matter. I have my girls in my arms. For this blissful fortnight, they are my entire world, and I intend to make the most of it.

"Say bye to your mum," I tell the girls, setting them down and hefting their glitter-strewn backpacks into the car.

Brianna crouches mechanically, brushing perfunctory kisses over their foreheads. "Be good, angels. Enjoy time with your father, alright?"

"Wait! We made you pictures for Christmas," June pipes up, rushing to her room and back, holding out slightly crumpled drawings from both girls.

Brianna takes them with a thin smile that doesn't reach her eyes. "They're lovely, my pets." She passes the artwork to Axel without a glance. "We'll put them on the fridge for when we get back, shall we?"

June's face falls a little as Axel stuffs the papers out of sight. I bite my tongue to stay civil; the girls don't need to see the anger simmering in me. I know whatever art they create for me during this visit will have places of pride displayed back at my house. For now, I just need to get them away, balanced, and happy. Brianna will always put herself first, and I refuse to let her damage claim more innocent victims.

"Okay, my loves, into the car," I say brightly, ushering the girls ahead of me. "We've got Christmas cookies to bake at Grandma's." That draws smiles and laughter again. As long as I'm here, Brianna's apathy won't dull their shine. Not in my presence.

THE LIVING ROOM IS STILL BEDECKED WALL TO WALL WITH evergreen boughs and cheery poinsettias giving off a festive scent. A few lone scraps of colored wrapping papers litter the floor, remnants from yesterday's frenzy of gifts and squealing girls. I nestle deeper into Mum's well-worn armchair as our dishes clink softly in the cozy kitchen-adjacent dining nook. Outside big, fluffy snowflakes drift lazily past lead-lined windows still dressed in charming Christmas fairy lights.

Mum soon joins me by the fireplace, porcelain teacup in hand, piercing gaze raking my scruffy appearance. "You look tired, pet." Her assessment thinly veils her constant disapproval.

"Well, managing a rock band these days requires keeping rockstar hours to stay in sync with the musicians." I shrug through a sip of Earl Grey that I wish to God was whisky.

"When are you going to get a real job and settle down? Give those sweet girls some stability? Lord knows Brianna can't or won't do it. And I won't be here forever to step in, you know." Mum's tone softens slightly with the latter part.

I clench my jaw, the old clash of wills rising. We

relive variations of this script every visit home. And while she's not wrong about Brianna, she knows better about me. Seeing the earnest care etched in her features, though, some of my defensiveness eases. She may repeatedly judge the shape of my existence, but ensuring my daughters' well-being drives it all. My voice loses some of its edge. "No one is ever truly prepared to become a parent. But I do the best I can."

"Gadding about to concerts and music festivals is no proper work for a man pushing middle age with daughters," she presses on, lowering her voice even more.

My stomach knots thinking of the woman an ocean away I'm currently doing a shit job of tending any connection with. But Mackenzie's dreams never included kids and minivans. I rake a hand roughly through my hair.

"I have, and ideally, I always will provide for Hayley and June directly. As for nesting," I shrug, "Maybe it'll happen, but 'stability' isn't my strong suit. Never has been. You know this."

Mum's nostrils flare, but before tensions boil over, June tugs my sleeve. "Daddy, can we play my new Candyland game from Santa?" My mother's criticisms fade away as I meet my little girl's hopeful gaze. I may constantly wrestle with shortcomings, but being a Dad is one identity I've gotten right.

"Absolutely, darling heart," I tickle June mercilessly until she squeals and runs off to fetch the game.

No matter what failures I perpetuate with the other women in my disaster zone of a love life, my girls will always be my guiding lights.

My hand reflexively goes to the front left pocket of my jeans, my thumb sliding over the phone concealed within. Mackenzie's 'Merry Christmas' text from yesterday morning still glares up at me, the platitude underscored by the last few days of strain and silence. My inept, 'Happy Christmas, hope you're well,' reply late last night sent after the girls fell asleep mocks me in its complete inadequacy.

I know it's only prolonging the inevitable. She'll learn the truth about June and Hayley soon enough. It's inevitable. It'll surely be a death knell sounding over anything real developing between us. Still, I masochistically torture myself, grasping at these last scraps of connection. I'm well beyond mere avoidance or denial. I bloody yearn to stop the entire fucking world, rewind, and start fresh with all truths laid bare from the beginning.

My spiraling internal musings break off as June bounds over clutching Candyland. As her sweet chatter fills the room, I am desperate to imprint every detail of this joyous time together. Who knows how many more I have before this house of cards collapses on top of me, breaking me down.

For now, I force brighter smiles. Listen closer. There is still goodness to be found in each passing moment, however fleeting. I owe my daughters that indefinitely where possible.

With June now beckoning me eagerly to play, it seems the annual clash with my Mum has reached yet another stalemate. We mean well in disparate ways. As I settle onto the carpet to play games, I meet Mum's gaze briefly. A sort of tired peace offering. She worries, and she loves. The rest we navigate one game night at a time.

I gulp the last mouthful of lukewarm coffee as I stare blearily at my laptop screen. The droning pulse of my neighbor's tasteless annual techno New Year's playlist seeps through my apartment walls, fraying what few brain cells haven't already flatlined from slogging through band accounting and revenue statements.

Leaning back with a joint-popping stretch, I observe the sunny California skies outside with mounting dread. Year-end reporting will be the death of me. My least favorite part of managing Murderous Crows. But Blackmore expects properly filed records, so I resign myself to the work. At least the band's tour did damn good numbers this year. And, the festival was surprisingly profitable despite the weather.

Of course, that makes Ian flash through my mind,

and I sit up curiously, wondering if Ian knows he needs to submit end-of-year paperwork too. He's an industry veteran but was on the artistry and talent scouting side before. Surely the label debriefed him. But knowing that chaotic band, plans probably got lost in the turmoil.

My hand hovers over my phone for a beat. I haven't reached out since his, 'Happy-Christmas-hope-you're-well,' text. The gulf between us lately has me second-guessing everything. I've been giving him space, knowing he's a million time zones away. Maybe I should check in, and make sure the crash course in band admin stuck? Give us a chance to actually talk?

Before I overthink too much, I fire off a quick text.

> ME: Hey rockstar, you getting your year-end reporting done on schedule? Holler if you need band management crash course number two.

I've barely set my phone down, resigned to the silence continuing when it unexpectedly chimes Ian's custom ringtone. I snatch it back up quickly.

> Ian: Reports? What reports should I be doing??

My pulse kicks up a notch at the first direct contact we've had since our holiday pleasantries. I pause before typing back. Torn between relief at his reply and uncertainty swirling heavier now that an actual conversation has opened. Still, business talk feels like neutral enough territory for testing the waters.

> Me: End of year accounting. Summary of tour and merch profits, expenses & payouts to everyone. Sorry, thought Eliza would have prepped you for this stuff. Sending you the templates I use.

I tap send on the standard issue Excel sheets we use every year, watching the little loading bar anxiously. Our text bubbles fall still and silent again. Until at last, those delightful three wiggling dots pop up signaling he's typing. I try futilely to temper the eyebrow-raising hope that sparks in me.

It's just routine paperwork, Mackenzie. That's likely all this exchange means.

But still...he wrote back. It's a start.

I straighten up in my desk chair, willing a substantive reply to manifest itself into being. I'm not at all ready for the short reply.

> IAN: Got it. Thanks.

Wow. That was...something.

My gaze falls on the small gift box resting on my desk corner. I'd picked it up back in Vegas while doing some holiday shopping with Chelsie. She encouraged me to get Ian a little something, and well, when I saw them in the store, I had to buy them. Despite myself, I internally smile at what his reaction will be to the gift.

But that was all before things took this unexpected silent turn between us. And as I now stare glumly out at the LA skyline, I debate whether I should even still give it to him.

Who knows if a small gift can overcome the emotional distance that's opened up? Is it me? Did I do something to push him away? Or is this just me discovering how Ian truly is in real life? Non-communicative and distant. It doesn't feel like him. It feels all kinds of wrong.

Then again, it's quite possible the holidays likely monopolized his time at home in England with family. And it's not like we owe each other anything.

We never talked about it.

Why didn't we talk about it? Why didn't we plan out our next steps? Where this was going between us?

Everyone hates labels, but god damnit, I need to know where I stand. Something more happened between us in Aspen. I know I'm not alone in thinking that, and it scared the shit out of me. But, I'm still here. I'm still trying. Did it scare off Ian that much, that he's retreating now?

The hero I know who saved me on the slopes, saved a cat frozen in the snow, and almost barehandedly saved a music festival cannot be the same man I'm texting now. My heart doesn't want to believe it.

Maybe I shouldn't expect anything back. But damn, isn't that what we all want? To be loved the way we love?

Is this love? Jesus Christ.

I make a decision - I'll hold onto it a bit longer. See what unfolds after the chaos of the holidays subsides and regular day-to-day activity returns. Once he's back in LA, I'll be able to see where we stand. We'll be able to talk face-to-face and see what each of us is willing to offer the other. I'm determined to figure this out.

New year, new relationship, new me who wants to actually fight for this one.

I set the gift aside with a tentative resolution kindling inside. Here's to new beginnings, I think wryly.

Wouldn't that be nice?

Mackenzie's texts about year-end reports instantly transform my leisurely hotel morning into a shitstorm. With the girls currently starfished on the carpet watching cartoons, I scramble to access the band accounts on my phone. But blotchy cell service and this hotel's sketchy Wi-Fi are making a mockery of productivity. I'm hamstrung by my limited technology here.

I need my LA home office setup, plus my laptop rather than just a mobile screen if I stand any chance of tackling the paperwork storm now brewing on my horizon. I really didn't think I'd need a laptop for this trip. It's the fucking holidays after all.

Obviously, I should have known better.

"Ladies, how do you fancy a surprise trip to visit Stormy kitty?" I ask brightly. June and Hayley instantly perk up. I'd shown them pictures of the rescue cat I adopted, and the updates from the neighbors, and they haven't stopped asking about her.

"Yes! Yes! Yes!" The girls jump up in unison. Two peas in a kitty-loving pod.

I dial Brianna to inform her of my changed plans. As expected, she acquiesces easily to me taking the girls back with me, her holiday tropical bliss uninterrupted. No surprise there.

Within hours, we've said farewell to Grandma, grabbed the girls' passports from Brianna's house thanks to a neighbor with a key, and bundled onto an early flight across the pond. The girls vibrate with excitement in the jet bridge line. I paste on an equally enthusiastic face to match as we board, quelling my rising anxiety. Maybe a transatlantic haul ending with cat introductions and frantic band paperwork amidst solo parenting isn't the most prudent decision...but the die has been cast now.

We live and die by our rash decisions, don't we?

As we reach cruising altitude, I glance down to where Hayley and June have already curled up, sleepy against my side. Come what may outside of my control, at least we're in this adventure together. The only reliable variable in my universe. I smooth back an errant wisp of June's baby-fine hair and smile softly to myself. Family first, always, and forever. We'll sort the rest soon enough.

Hayley squeals with delight as Stormy the kitten gingerly bats at a catnip-stuffed mouse while June makes explosion sounds. Home only two days and my daughters have turned traitor, utterly enthralled by the feline addition to our family. I've become a non-entity in their world for the time being, but Stormy is basking in the sudden spotlight she finds herself in. I can't complain though, their joy overrides my stress.

I crack my neck side to side, the numbers on my laptop screen blurring together. Profits, expenses, payouts - more figures than I can keep straight under any looming accountant's microscope.

I'm drowning here.

Realizing I'm in over my head, I dial Blackmore's VP, Eliza Kerr when the girls head off to play. No answer.

"Eliza, it's Ian. Sorry for the short notice, but I could use guidance completing Chaos Fuel's year-end reports by the deadline. Been scrambling since Mackenzie messaged me that these were due. And I'm working with scattered receipts from previous managers. Please ring me back regarding an extension? Maybe? Cheers."

My phone lights up quickly with Eliza's return call. I maneuver a now-sleeping Stormy from my lap to place her next to me on the couch. She's obviously exhausted from the unfamiliar vigorous playtime. I slip onto the porch, closing the glass door behind me quietly.

"Eliza, thanks for getting back to me. I genuinely apologize for the last-minute holiday ask here."

She interrupts my rambling. "No need to apologize, Ian. I should have personally ensured you had the report templates before the holiday madness kicked in."

I run a hand through my hair, breathing out in relief. "I'm just grateful for your help navigating this. Being back stateside in LA is already making things easier in terms of accessing the financial records. I just needed my laptop. But the records are scattered..."

"You're back in California already?" Surprise colors Eliza's voice. "Weren't you meant to be in London through mid-January?"

"Yeah, that laptop need I mentioned changed my plans. It's alright though, the girls are with me. We decided visiting the new kitten took priority over London rain and my mum's grilling on about when I'll get a proper career." I let out a tired chuckle.

Eliza graciously grants me an extension to file the reports, and I vow to get them to her by the new deadline. We extend New Year's greetings before hanging up.

I can figure this shit out; I just need more time.

Man, that sounds so familiar. I just need more time... for everything.

When did time become such an enemy to me? I suddenly want to go back in time, stop time, beat time. It's a race that I'm losing miserably.

And soon enough, my girls will need to go home to England, so I'll lose them in a way. And heaven knows, I'll lose Mackenzie any second now, if I haven't already with my distance.

We live and die by our rash decisions.

Bloody hell, we do.

My imported dark roast is barely tingling my taste buds when Eliza Kerr's name flashes insistently across my phone screen. I contemplate ignoring the call. Blackmore's VP contacting me on New Year's Eve likely means only one thing - more work.

With a resigned sigh, I accept. "This is Mackenzie."

"Mackenzie, it's Eliza. I hope I'm not interrupting any early New Year's celebrations..."

I snort. Unless binging Supernatural on Netflix with a microwaved lunch counts as a celebration. "All good. What's up?"

"Well, it's Ian. Turns out no one properly prepared the poor man on the required band accounting before the holiday madness. But I just spoke with him. He decided to return to LA early to tackle things from his home. I thought maybe since you're an expert at those you could lend him a hand? I know you've already sent the templates..."

I wince in sympathy, knowing firsthand that frantic year-end feeling, but my heart sinks. He didn't tell me he was back. I quickly compose myself, as usual, and turn back on my professionalism. "Of course, I'd be happy to help. I can offer Ian guidance on getting the reports finalized now that he's back stateside."

"That would be amazing. I gave him an extension but having your expertise could really ensure he submits error-free." Eliza lets out a relieved breath. "Especially with the new chaos of a recently adopted cat too apparently? I don't know how you people juggle all of these things, honestly. I can't keep an artificial plant alive, and I don't even travel as much as you guys do."

I feel an unconscious smile form. Stormy does happen to be a special cat to me after our separate misadventures in the Aspen mountains. Both of us were rescued by Ian. The thought warms me, despite my hurt. "Well, now I definitely have to visit and check on that little survivor. And I'll give Ian an assist getting back on track with the paperwork."

After getting more details, and hanging up with Eliza, emotions war within me. On one hand, that sharp hurt simmers that Ian didn't tell me himself that he was back in LA. Yet I'm already grabbing my keys, intent on checking on the sweet rescue cat, and evidently offering accounting assistance to my floundering colleague, too.

Colleague.

If I'm honest with myself, it's more that I'm determined to finally have it out with Ian face-to-face. Chelsie was right back in Vegas. I need to lay it all out on the table, and let the cards fall where they may. Are we just colleagues now? Can I even do that after everything that's happened between us?

I'm starting to think I care far more than I should about this man.

I harden my resolve as I grab Ian's gift off the desk. There's only one way to find out. I refuse to let this pull between us vanish so easily without at least putting up a fight.

Time for answers. I need to know where I stand.

"Girls, c'mon, I'm begging you, Daddy needs to focus," I plead in vain over the tornado of scattered receipts, laptop, and Hayley and June's giggling couch cushion fort disaster area. They're lost in some fantasy land only kid brains can dream up.

I rub my eyes hard, longing for their giddiness. Eliza's reporting deadline extension is just a leaky dam against a flood of paperwork I'm drowning in at this point. What temporary insanity made me think flying overseas alone with my daughters would relax this workload avalanche? Though, to be fair, my thinking hasn't exactly been straight lately.

The loud chime of the doorbell jars me alert just as Hayley tumbles more decorative pillows from the couch. I freeze, pulse jackhammering. We aren't expecting anyone. June grins impishly from atop the sofa back. "Daddy's in trouble..."

"Trouble? Me?" I scoff playfully. "I'm not the one that practically dismantled the couch to make a cat condo."

I ruffle her hair on the way to see what fresh hell my horrible judgment has delivered now. Maybe it's the millions of cat toys I ordered from the internet in a jet-lagged haze last night.

Then, I stop dead as I glimpse through the front door's stained glass.

No no no...

I turn the lock, pulse pounding. Mackenzie being here cannot be real, despite knowing this reckoning always lurked around the corner. The air leaves my body. But there's no hiding the two wild-haired little girls now flanking me, toys in hand.

"Who's this, Daddy?" Hayley asks, always curious.

I meet Mackenzie's wide eyes, shock rooting me in place. Nothing to do but let the ugly truth flood out.

"Girls, this is my...friend, Mackenzie." I gesture helplessly. "Mackenzie, meet my daughters, Hayley and June."

"Happy New Year, ladies!" Mackenzie greets them with an admirably steady voice given her deer-in-headlights expression just moments ago.

The girls chorus excited hellos, June clinging shyly

to my leg while Hayley approaches Mackenzie and takes her hand, always the social butterfly. "Look! We got a kitty, Stormy! Wanna meet her? She's daddy's friend too."

Mackenzie's eyes flash to mine as I rake a hand through my hair. "Ah, yes, Stormy." She's already nodding slowly, not breaking my gaze. "We've...met before actually."

I wince, imagining the avalanche of questions brewing behind her overly polite smile. "Look, Mackenzie..." I start, desperately trying to find something to say about all this. Still, no words come to explain away my lies.

"Oh, um...here." Still taken off guard, Mackenzie passes the wrapped present over with an awkward shrug, allowing my effervescent daughter to continue guiding her down the hall.

Hayley tugs on a rather shellshocked Mackenzie while I follow in equal fashion, staring numbly at the neatly gift-wrapped box now feeling like a grenade in my hands.

"Oooh, what'd ya get, Daddy?" June hops excitedly from foot to foot as I fall onto the now-uncushioned couch.

I force enthusiasm into my tone for her benefit, even though I'm still too stunned to feel a damned thing. "Well let's see then, shall we?" Gently I unwrap a stunning set of the *If* book series.

"You might want to wait..." Mackenzie says, reaching out towards me from across the room as if trying to stop a tornado with sheer force of will, but it's too late. Pandora's figurative box has already been opened. In more ways than one.

My throat thickens as June traces the ornate font of the book titles with one small finger.

If.

An entire bloody series of *If* books, including the one we stumbled upon in the cabin in Aspen. The one that broke both of our barriers down. Well, mostly. What I left out is right in front of us; one next to me, and one next to her.

Seeing that particular volume among them feels like a glaring condemnation now.

"They're so pretty!" June enthuses, oblivious to the hollowness opening within me. "Daddy loves books. He reads us all kinds of stories."

I look helplessly across the room where Hayley continues introducing a variety of topics to a hero-ically patient Mackenzie. "Look, I am so very sor-"

My stammering apology cuts off as Hayley scoops up a yawning Stormy, and barrels excitedly across the room. "Stormy remembers Mackenzie too. Did you see? They're friends."

I meet Mackenzie's conflicted eyes as she follows Hayley and gives Stormy a gentle stroke that belies her calm facade.

"We are friends," she says, giving me a pointed

look. Her face is serious, and kind, but her brilliant violet eyes are unreadable. I can see the machinery at work on her emotions but don't know what to expect from it.

What does it all mean?

"You didn't say thank you," Hayley reminds me, taking Stormy back to the impromptu cat condo with June trailing behind. "That's not polite. Grandma says you should always say thank you, even if you don't like what you got."

Rightfully chastised, I announce, "Of course, Your grandmother is right." I look back up at Mackenzie. "Thank you. This was very thoughtful of you. *These books* are very thoughtful. I'll cherish them."

If anything, I'm not lying now. I *will* treasure these books, even though I'm sure she's going to leave this house and probably never speak to me again, I will covet these books forever.

"You're welcome," she says, pulling on a braid, suddenly awkward and nervous. She's rattled. Of course, she is.

I need to explain.

"What happened to your leg?" June asks before I can even start. She timidly points to Mackenzie's brace.

"Oh, this?" Mackenzie wiggles her booted foot. She's maneuvering smoothly without crutches, which is great to see. I hope it means she's on the mend. "I had an accident skiing not too long ago, and slid smack dab into a pole, and your daddy actually rescued me before a big blizzard hit."

"He did?" both girls ask, suddenly surprised I would do such a thing. I'm almost offended.

"He did," Mackenzie nods, still not giving away any emotion on the subject. I can't read her.

"Well, my Daddy's a good skier," Hayley announces, finally coming to the defense of my bruised pride. "He probably swooped right in there and skied you right to safety. Just like he did with Stormy."

Mackenzie's eyes tighten ever so slightly. "Well, he called the *real* rescue squad for me, which is heroic enough."

I can't take it anymore and need to interject before my daughters paint her into a corner that she doesn't want to be in.

"Girls, keep an eye on Stormy for me while I talk outside with Mackenzie, okay?" I set the books aside and move to the patio door, beckoning Mackenzie to follow me, which thankfully, she does.

The girls luckily don't respond. They're already wrapped up back in their land of make-believe with Stormy. I wish internally I could go there too, but I've got to deal with this situation.

I slide the patio door shut behind us with a gentle click. Mackenzie faces me, arms crossed protectively over her chest, intense eyes turbulent with a brewing storm. I shove restless hands into my pockets. The air lies still and heavy around us, an expectant jury awaiting my plea.

"Mackenzie, I..." Words fail and falter again under her searching gaze. I swallow dryly and start again hoarsely. "After your accident, we bonded so intensely. But when you talked before about not being mother material, not seeing kids in your future..."

I trail off and rake both hands roughly through my hair, grasping for the right thing to say. There is no right thing. "God this sounds horrible, but I didn't know how you'd react. Or that it could ever turn serious between us. I just didn't mention having them at first and then felt trapped as my feelings for you grew-"

"Don't." Mackenzie stops my rambling with a single cutting word, eyes flashing. "Don't you dare pin this on things I confided back when I thought I knew you." She looks away, jaw tightening. "You had a thousand chances to tell me, Ian. At any point, you could've trusted me with the truth."

The weight of her words sinks like stones in my gut. She's right. Of course, she's fucking right. This mess lies squarely on me alone. I drag my eyes up to meet her fiery gaze again, shaking my head helplessly.

"You deserve so much more. I'm so very sorry, Mackenzie. For all of it. For not being honest from the start. And for hurting you now in the process." My chest feels hollowed out and raw admitting that truth at last, but we both deserve that honesty, even if it's much too little much too late.

I take a slight step closer, desperate for her to truly feel my remorse to the bone.

"Mackenzie, I was a damn coward and fool," I admit rawly. "I should have shouted about the girls from the bloody rooftops from day one with you. You have a heart deep enough to encompass anything life throws at you. I know that. I saw it in how you cared for that helpless cat...for *me* when I know I hardly deserved your time or attention at all."

I risk another half-step into her space, close enough now to see the pulse hammering in her slender throat. When she doesn't immediately recoil, a reckless hope flares inside of me. I lift my palm to hover tentatively before grazing her arm. Our first physical connection since Aspen rekindles my nerve endings.

"Please believe how sorry I am," I urge hoarsely. "I never dreamed my past could collide with a future containing you until suddenly there you were during that blizzard. You think I saved you, but you were saving me right back. I haven't felt anything close to what I feel for you. Ever. I thought feelings like this were impossible. After that, hiding it felt like my one and only option. I knew you'd find out, and when you did, it would devastate both of us. And regardless of the million times I almost told you about them, I couldn't find the right words. Couldn't think of anything to explain what an ass I am. Because losing this terrifying, breathless thing growing between us felt even worse."

I slowly meet her conflicted eyes once more, allowing the naked truth to shine through mine in return. "I know my actions don't show it yet...but I lo-"

I catch myself just before the massive confession tumbles out, unsure if laying that depth of feeling upon her now might shatter this fragile moment irrevocably. And honestly unsure if it's the right word for what I'm feeling. My heart and mind are a fucking mess right now. I change course mid-word.

"...I care for you, truly I do. Far more than makes sense after our short time knowing one another." I give a self-deprecating huff of laughter. "Hell, we hardly know one another at all, except *here*."

I tap two fingers lightly over the thudding pulse in her wrist. "Here is where I witnessed who you are deep down; focused, funny, caring. And bloody brave with that cracked leg of yours. Hell, even in the face of my spectacular cowardice..."

I trail off, shaking my head. "I don't know what future pains my omission has cost me, cost *us*. But I'm praying to gods, planets, whatever forces exist that we might find a way through this shitstorm that I've created somehow." My eyes sear fiercely into hers now, willing her to see through to the tattered remains of my soul. "Just tell me how to fix this, Mackenzie. I'm begging you. Whatever I need to do. I can't lose..."

You.

My heart screams the word, but my lips won't risk the plunge. So, instead, I stare helplessly, awaiting the ultimate jury's verdict on my redemption.

Please tell me it's not over.

My head spins as I stare sightlessly out at the LA skyline. Dinner leftovers congeal, forgotten on my kitchen counter. Hours have passed in a blur since I left Ian's place, yet my mind churns in relentless circles.

I press the heels of both hands against my eyes until colors burst across the darkness. It would almost be laughable if my heart wasn't so bruised by this secret double life Ian has been leading that I stumbled upon so accidentally.

Those sweet little girls with their bouncing curls, cobbled cat condo, and art projects littering the floor. That damn cat winding happily between all their books and crayons. It looked for all the world like the family portrait I never dared wish for.

And now it's cracked straight through the center,

fissured by Ian's omission. What the fuck do I do with all this?

My phone blinks with another text. Ian's tenth since I left him and the girls. Begging for a response, for a chance to regain my trust, piece by piece if need be. He even joked about running a background check on him for other stray family members around the globe to prove his honesty now.

I huff a watery almost-laugh. Ian the family man. It's still such a startling image for the brooding ex-rockstar I thought I knew. But one that fits him like a missing puzzle piece now that it's slid into place. Now that I've seen it in person.

I just need some time alone to think, to absorb it all without him pleading those heartbreaking eyes at me. *Soon. We'll talk again soon*, I promise myself, picking up my phone to tap a brief reply.

I bundle under a blanket on my balcony facing downtown, nursing a glass of wine as fireworks burst in glittering arcs over the skyline. Red and gold flash vibrant against the darkness. What should be a sight full of joy and bright hope for the unfolding new year is now steeped in melancholy for me.

My phone buzzes, lighting up with Chelsie's face. I lift it hesitantly.

"Happy New Year!" we both chorus at once, the echo of other years together warming me slightly against the cool night air.

Ever attuned to my rhythms, Chelsie pauses after

our ritual well-wishing. "Everything okay, hon? You sound off."

I smile despite myself. Is there anything that gets past her? I take a larger gulp of merlot before answering carefully. "Just thinking through some heavy realizations about relationships. And what I actually want mine to look like in this new year and beyond."

"Realizations about a certain British manager we know and maybe love?" she coaxes gently.

My breath leaves in a rush. So much for careful vagaries. "He has kids, Chels. Two adorable little daughters he conveniently forgot to mention until I accidentally met them this afternoon."

Her soft gasp echoes my own swirling shock and betrayal. As colorful explosions continue to paint the skyline with light, I unravel it all to her.

When I finish, Chelsie lets silence land comfortably between us for a time. Finally, softly, she says, "The Mackenzie Roberts I know doesn't run when shit gets real."

She's not wrong there. I don't. But I also don't stand for bullshit either. I'm still wading through what this actually is, and how I feel about it.

When we hang up, my phone lights up again instantly with an incoming video call from Logan and Skyler. I paste on a smile before answering.

"Happy New Year, Mr. and Mrs. Edwards!" I cheer, as their glowing faces fill my screen, party hats tilted

jauntily. I'm able to mostly listen, interjecting occasional "Wows" over their epic New Year's party story,
before getting passed off to Remy and his fiancée
Monroe.

More enthusiastic New Year's tidings and tales
ensue with each band member's trade-off. I *ooh* and
aah in the right places, tamping down my envy at their
thrilled drunken faces. My mind can't help but wander
to Ian celebrating with his sweet girls.

Does he feel as lonely as I do right now?

"Earth to Mackenzie..." Jake's smooth voice jars me
from my internal grumblings. "You get to flyin' solo
tonight or what?"

I smooth my features quickly, reverting to my
earlier white lie. "Oh, no. I've just been fighting some
nasty flu bug all day. Finally on the mend though. No
worries."

We exchange more well wishes before I'm able to
beg off for more rest. As I set down my dark phone, the
bright fireworks still blooming in the distance seem to
mock my descent into depression.

Happy New Year to me.

"Ten...nine...eight..."

The TV's New Year's countdown echoes faintly as Hayley and June fight against heavy eyelids. We're camped on the reassembled couch buried under blankets. My little nuggets are determined to fist-bump the new year despite the knockout punches of our combined jet lag.

I sweep Hayley's messy curls off her face as she yawns big enough to catch flies. My throat clutches and a familiar face invades my thoughts, crowding out the sparkly ball poised to drop onscreen. Is Mackenzie also nursing a drink somewhere, with only my bullshit betrayal to toast to come midnight?

"...seven...six..."

June's small hand slips into mine, tugging me back. Despite all of my wheel-spinning regrets, last year isn't changing. Its hangovers are nearly passed out here beside me.

Maybe someday I'll be forgiven. But midnight doesn't bring a magic time machine with it. It's just us three musketeers welcoming the mystery of whatever the new year wants to throw down.

Forward we go, ready or not.

The girls mumble sleepy, "...three ...two ...one ...Happy New Year!" We share soft pecks on the cheek in our pint-sized wolfpack.

It'll do.

A MID-MORNING RAP ON THE DOORFRAME MAKES ME GLANCE up from my laptop balancing precariously on the arm of the sofa. My neighbor Marisha smiles kindly, her own girls already squeezing past her to clamber inside.

"I come bearing reinforcements as requested."

I rise swiftly, relief and gratitude washing over me that small crises, while innocuous, can still be handled so friendly between neighbors. Marisha happily agreed to watch the girls for a few hours when I confided to her that I needed to discuss some delicate matters with a friend. Bless her for intuiting my turmoil without prying.

"Thanks so much for doing this," I smile, bending

to kiss each of my girls goodbye before straightening awkwardly.

"Take your time, and enjoy your visit with your friend." Her knowing look needs no response.

Marisha waves away my thanks as the girls chatter animatedly about their impending playdate. Within moments the house seems to exhale into a stillness around me. I check my phone compulsively as I grab my keys.

Just then Mackenzie's name flashes onto the screen and I scramble to answer. "Hello, yes, I'm just heading out now."

Her responding voice jacks up my already racing pulse when she confirms our oceanfront meeting spot. I slide behind the wheel, the ignition firing to life. "Brilliant, I'll be there shortly," I assure her, wheels already churning towards reconciliation, or whatever this is going to be.

Maybe it will just be an ending made kinder for finally being honest? I don't know how much longer I can keep holding my breath.

I'll hold it however long it takes, though.

T he salt air kisses my cheeks, carrying that familiar briny vibe that I love about LA. I feel myself standing at an edge here, and not just the ocean. A metaphorical edge that has grown closer since I met Ian.

Truth is I've teetered at this line for years, never daring to fully plunge into love's choppy waters. Always opting to kick my feet to push me back to firm land, and somehow find solace on a lone rock, stubborn against those wild waves.

Love wasn't for me.

I work in rock 'n roll. Nothing is permanent. Everything is temporary. Especially relationships. I've seen it firsthand. At least, up until my guys found their partners. Once that started happening, and then meeting and falling for Ian like I did, my mind started to change.

But after meeting his daughters? Talk about a tail-spin. I don't even know which way is up anymore.

Yet some intense magnetic pull lately keeps drawing me back to thoughts of him. Maybe we can keep it together if I can get my heart and mind in sync with all of his secrets. Or, I might have to say painful goodbyes if it's too little too late.

I still don't know what I want.

"Mackenzie..." Ian's voice sounds behind me and I pivot slowly, drinking in his beloved scruffy jawline as he ambles toward me on the boardwalk, looking both weighted down and freer than when I saw him yesterday. His normally sparkling eyes are tired.

My equilibrium shifts. I correct my earlier thought - we already plunged into the deep end of this. I know it and he does too. The choice now is whether to battle against the waves we've created or drown in what's been churned up.

I remember a prior thought I had about Logan getting married to Skyler: Learning to swim or just learning not to drown.

I want to learn to swim.

He stops an arm's length away, hopefulness pinging beneath the regret still plain across the features I've mentally traced for countless restless hours since my world flipped upside down.

"Hey...thank you for coming...and for this chance."

My eyes catch briefly on his mouth and skitter away. One wrong move and muscle memory might kick in, recalling too clearly the megawatt voltage of his kiss. I shift my gaze seaward and anchor there. But through the salty haze, my reckless heart knows what it wants most.

Ian searches my face while I sift through my swirling thoughts. Finally, I just sigh. "Why couldn't you trust me? We've known each other for a long time, Ian. Sure, not like we do now, but I thought things had clicked deeper between us."

He scrubs a hand over his scruff in frustration. "You deserved that truth and more. I was a total coward about coming clean immediately. But I won't apologize for my daughters. I'll never apologize for them. I just should have had more faith that you'd understand all of me, including my being a father. Once we really bonded, I just couldn't bear losing whatever this might be." He waves at the air between us, his voice cracking with emotion.

"But the longer you waited, the worse it got," I snap off a nearby length of driftwood angrily. "If you would have told me earlier, maybe--"

"You think I don't know that?" Ian combs both hands roughly through his hair. "I hated myself more and more every bloody day I went without telling you. But the dream of you, of us, was too attractive." His eyes burn intensely into mine again. "You're like this flame I can't stop circling closer to, common sense be damned. I fucked up, alright? I know I did."

I hug my middle at his admission, rocking back slightly. "So where does that leave us now?" I whisper finally. "Now that the truth's burned down everything between us?"

He closes the distance tentatively, his hand coming up to graze my cheek. "That's what I'm praying with everything in me isn't the case." His eyes trail over my features with a reverence that gives me those oh-so-tempting unfamiliar flutters. "Tell me the damage isn't irreparable, Mackenzie. I swear I'll spend forever trying to make this up to you."

Ian tilts my chin up gently, remorse and longing in his green eyes. "I know I don't deserve this after the trust I shattered. But you make me want to be better, Mackenzie. With you, I see a future I stopped imagining for myself a long time ago. I mean it down to my soul. What we started meant everything to me. It still does."

He wraps his hand behind my neck, "I understand if that's too hard to believe after...well, everything." His eyes squeeze shut, pained. "But what we have between us - it's the truest thing I've ever felt. I should've had faith you'd understand all of me, including my past. Including my girls."

His thumb traces my bottom lip tentatively and I sway closer, my walls crumbling. I'm losing the war with what I thought were my impenetrable defenses.

"Give this a chance?" he whispers roughly. "Please? Give me a chance to rebuild what I recklessly fucked up? I swear here and now, and as many times as I have to, I'll never stop making amends, or letting you into every hidden corner of my life that you want in on."

My reservations want to linger and hold me back, but in his touch, his voice, and his pleading look, I recognize the only man who made me feel truly seen. I can't help but press a kiss to his palm and his breath shudders out in fragile hope.

"I believe you," I whisper, walls collapsing as I grip his shirt, tugging on him firmly. Our lips meet hungrily at last, that electric familiarity between us flickering to life again.

We pull apart, and my hands slide up his chest. I fist them there, anchors against the dizzying freefall now happening. "You damn well better not hide anything from me ever again," I warn breathlessly. Heart hammering, I drag him back to me. Sparks instantly detonate as our lips meet once again.

This could be the completely wrong decision to make, but damn, if it all goes to shit, it will go down in brilliant flames.

The knot I've carried around for endless days finally loosens in my chest as Mackenzie and I stroll, fingers interlaced, along the boardwalk of the beach after making amends. When I first arrived, as tense as an overly-tuned guitar string for our discussion, all of my pleas and apologies hit me at once, and everything spilled out in a rush.

I should feel empty after baring my soul so much, finally releasing everything I've been holding back. Instead, I feel full for the first time.

Complete.

By some miracle, cracks of light penetrated both our armor. Now unfettered joy fills me with warmth, and it's almost as dizzying as New Year's champagne bubbles, leaving me grateful but determined to keep us moving forward.

I sweep my thumb over her knuckles. "So, you met my little troublemakers yesterday during that ambush of yours."

Mackenzie's laugh lifts on the breeze. "They're really sweet, Ian." Her expression gentles. "June's shy excitement touring me through their artwork was precious. And Hayley showing me how she plays with Stormy..." Amusement glints in her eyes. "You've really got some great kids there."

Pride swells in my chest. "They're my earth and sun. And they already adore you." I hesitate briefly as an idea pops into my head. "In the spirit of new beginnings, would you consider an outing with the three of us? No pressure, but just...so we can merge worlds a bit? Get to know each other?"

Her features relax into a sincere smile that hits me straight in my heart. "I'd really like that." Her fingers tighten around mine as our footsteps align stride for stride, even with her slight limp. I have no problem adjusting to match her cadence.

In all things.

"Bye Marisha!" Hayley and June call, barreling out the neighbor's front door once we arrive to pick them up. "Where are we going, Daddy?"

I scoop them into a bear hug amidst a stream of questions. "Ah ah, your adventure's a surprise."

Then June spots Mackenzie in the car. "You're coming too?" she squeals, wriggling free to dash ahead.

"I convinced your new friend to show us one of her favorite places today," I wink, securing car seat buckles, and enjoying how my daughters are already embracing Mackenzie's presence.

Hayley tugs my arm eagerly. "Is it the zoo? Or rainbow ice cream land?"

I laugh. "I'm not telling. But maybe Miss Mackenzie knows..."

"The movies?" Hayley asks, joining June in grilling an amused Mackenzie from the back seat.

"Think we should keep making them guess until we get there?" Mac asks cheekily. I feel my smile widen seeing her shine so effortlessly with my girls. This New Year's Day is beginning on an optimistic upswing.

I absofuckinglutely love it.

As I drive, the girls vibrate with conspiracy theories, the undercurrent of playful chatter already flowing smoother with Mackenzie here than entire strained visits with my own mum and ex. My entire being seems to settle.

This simply feels right.

"Can we get our faces painted? Please, please, please?" Hayley tugs insistently at my hand as we pass the face art kiosk in Knott's Berry Farm, already bustling with transformed children sporting tiger stripes and butterfly wings.

I chuckle, glancing at Mackenzie to gauge her interest. She grins down at my eager daughter. "You know, temporary tattoos could be pretty fun too..." She winks up at me with a shrug of her shoulder. "Just saying."

Mackenzie has the girls utterly enraptured displaying her intricate ink. She shows them the flock of ravens silhouetted against a stunning purple sky on her inner forearm.

June's eyes round into awed saucers. "I want birdies just like you!"

"Oooh, me too!" Hayley confirms, then scrunches her nose, thoughtfully examining my fading punk tattoos. "But I think maybe I want a kitty for Stormy instead."

Soon they're settled into chairs, solemnly flipping through tattoo booklets while Mackenzie and I admire the samples displayed on the walls. My heart swells as the artists transfer my daughters' careful selections onto their small arms.

Temporarily, of course.

When finished, the girls gleefully compare their body art: June with a small raven flock flying up her wrist, and Hayley sporting a prowling black cat that remarkably looks a lot like Stormy.

"Now we match you AND Daddy!" Hayley announces proudly, grabbing Mackenzie's hand as we walk.

Mackenzie meets my undoubtedly soppy gaze, her own glinting playfully. "Aww."

Laughing, I pull her in for a quick kiss while the girls are distracted.

I could definitely get used to this.

Fireworks glitter in the night sky as Mackenzie gently sets a tuckered-out June into her car seat. I cradle a snoozing Hayley similarly amid stuffed animals won from various arcade games. The hero at work, yet again.

"They really did ring in the new year with a bang today, huh?" Mackenzie yawns with a soft smile, eyes tender on my daughters. I chuckle wearily, brushing a stray hair off Hayley's face.

"That they did," I agree. It's been an exhausting day, but worth every single second of it.

Together Mackenzie and I make quick work buckling seatbelts around slumbering little bodies. My own is pleasantly spent too after a day of panning for gold, kiddie-thrill rides, and silly old-timey snapshots capturing our first blended memories.

I close the back door softly once the girls are tucked in for our drive home, then pause, struck by the entire image. Just twenty-four little hours ago, these two separate spheres of my life felt fractured and frenetic.

Now Mackenzie stands haloed by the streetlamp's glow, looking for all the world like she belongs here - with an ice cream-stained sweatshirt and haywire hair falling from purple ponytails.

My heart stutters imagining more days and nights and years comprised of just such imperfect domestic bliss crafted together. If someone had told me yesterday my existence could radically transform overnight, I'd have laughed in their fucking face.

But now?

A single sunrise was all we needed.

I hover in the doorway of the girls' room, leaning on the frame to give my sore leg a rest and listen to Hayley and June's deep breathing as Ian finishes up a chapter in a bedtime story written by some famous British chef. My chest clutches watching this private dad moment. Ian makes silly character voices while the girls fight laughing at him with heavy eyelids while they lean against his chest.

It blows my mind how fast everything has changed. Just yesterday I stood angry on the patio of this house behind my own icy walls, convinced nothing excused Ian hiding his daughters' entire existence from me.

But June's excitement about art and Hayley's big opinions about music and cats thawed me out really fast. Too quickly I got suckered in by the mini-Ians.

And today, I glimpsed my own rare silly side reemerge seeing us all reflected in the fun house mirrors at the amusement park.

With last kisses to sleepy heads, Ian creeps out to the hall and slowly shuts the door. We make eye contact in this weird, suspended moment. A lot was dug up and patched today. What happens now as we stand at this fork in the road, that's actually a hallway outside his daughter's room?

I watch a kaleidoscope of expressions cross Ian's face. A lingering tenderness from the bedtime ritual shifts to something tentative, yet heated, as his eyes lock with mine.

He takes a half step closer in the shadowed hall-way, one hand lifting slowly to graze my hip before he seems to catch himself. I quirk a curious eyebrow as he lets out a self-conscious half-laugh instead, leaning in to press a gentle kiss to my forehead.

"They're out like lights already," he murmurs. "Let me just grab us a nightcap?"

I nod, lips tilting as I read the silent intention in his tired eyes. He's not quite ready to rush physical intimacy with his girls sleeping nearby. "Something strong to take the edge off all this, please," I joke lightly, following his familiar form toward the kitchen.

He pulls a decanter of amber liquid from a cabinet, raising it in query. "This scotch aged nearly as long as it took me to come clean..."

I let slip another small laugh at his wry tone, the knots inside me loosening. "Well, then it's aged well."

Maybe we'll just have a drink tonight, continuing to merge lives carefully first. There's plenty of time ahead of us now to explore all the new facets glittering temptingly beneath the surface.

Ian's expression softens as he pours two glasses. "Now then, how about a little light reading? For old time's sake?" He guides us back toward the crackling living room fireplace and my thoughts fly to our time at the cabin sitting by a fire just like this.

"Or, new times," I smile, raising my glass, exhaustion creeping in as Ian sits next to me and carefully pulls my legs onto his lap.

"How is your leg doing?" he asks, massaging my toes peeking out from the brace. "You braved an entire amusement park with this thing quite admirably."

I can't help but burst out a laugh. "Do you not recall me stopping for ice cream every twenty feet? It wasn't for the ice cream, it was so I could sit down for a minute. And I actually ended up wearing most of it." I glance down at my stained sweatshirt, imagining how haggard I must look right now.

His eyebrows raise. "Clever girl. And here I thought I'd finally discovered another weakness of yours. Besides hot chocolate, of course."

"Oh, you'll have to try harder than that."

A sly smile appears, and he leans over, barely brushing my lips. "I'd like to."

"Daddy, I'm thirsty," June's small voice calls from the hallway, and Ian pulls away quickly, composing himself.

I try my best to do the same before June rounds the corner, transferring my leg to the coffee table so he can get up.

He gives me a remorseful look that matches my own internal feelings. I have to remember that we have all the time in the world. And to be honest, we should be taking this slow. Apologetic words are still echoing in my brain, but I don't know that my heart heard them completely.

Patience. I need to find some patience.

And not just with Ian, but with myself too. I have a bad habit of always getting what I want because I make whatever it is happen. Without help. That's how I've learned to live and have been this way for a long fucking time. Now that there's another soul involved, or, in reality, three – I need to readjust my expectations. For everything, and everyone.

I grab one of the *If* books from the coffee table while Ian grabs June a drink of water, searching for a question to ask him. I could leave it to fate like we did last time, but I want to find something that really uncovers a truth about him that I don't know yet.

When he settles back next to me with an apology, he sweeps my legs over again and resumes his foot massage. "Now, where were we?"

"Alright Mr. Superhero, here's your first question. Ready?" I eye him over the book.

His shoulders slump as if in defeat and it's comical to see him pretend to hate this. "God that name is going to go to my head...I guess," he sighs deeply.

"If you could have one superpower what would it be?" I ask, slamming the book shut and handing it over to him.

"Time travel," he says without missing a beat, his tone serious.

"Time travel? Why?"

He stares solemnly at me for a moment before answering. "Do you know how many times I *literally* wished I could go back and tell you about my girls right away?"

"No...?"

"A lot." He gazes into the fire, lost in his own thoughts for a moment, regret still coloring his face.

"Ian, I understand now why you did it. You can stop beating yourself up about it." I reach over and rub his upper arm, trying to convey the truth in my own words. "I love your girls."

He turns, and his eyes are almost pained, but I can't entirely read his expression in the flickering firelight.

"Do you mean that?" His voice is soft, disbelieving. I can't believe he'd ever think I wouldn't or couldn't love his daughters.

"Of course, I do. They're amazing."

"So are you," he says, shaking his head a little. "I thought..."

"Yeah, well, you need to stop doing that. You're obviously no good at it, and it gets you into trouble," I say, feigning sternness. My smile breaks through my façade, and he finally laughs.

"You're right. It's a problem. I overthink everything."

"We do have that one thing in common, at least."

An eyebrow arches at me in question. "Just the one thing?"

Before I can reply, he's kissing me again, and I'm instantly lost in it. I've stopped fighting against this. It's useless to even try.

This man has my heart. And I don't miss it because I have his.

"Daddy, will Kenzie come with us on the airplane when we go back?"

I glance up from my laptop to see June watching Mackenzie gather the last receipts for the band reports across the room. Hayley looks up eagerly from where she's drawing at the coffee table.

"Um, well..." I catch Mackenzie's surprised eyes, temporarily stunned. We've only been dating - is *'dating'* even the right word here? For a matter of days. And reconciling from our past hurts a scant few longer. Would she even consider a trip with us?

Mackenzie opens her mouth but Hayley barrels on excitedly. "We could show her our play castle at Mummy's and wear pretty dresses! We could have tea parties every day!"

A slightly panicked laugh escapes before I interject

gently. "I don't know if Mackenzie is up for trips and tea parties, little love." I cringe internally, hoping I haven't made presumptions. "We'll just focus on getting you two back safe and sound for now, yeah?"

Mackenzie moves behind the girls, meeting my apprehensive gaze steadily. "Oh, I don't know. I haven't been to a tea party in a long time." Her smile is apprehensive but encouraging.

"Oh, we have tiaras too," Hayley announces, bouncing on her tiptoes now with excitement at the prospect of Mackenzie's inclusion. "I know exactly which one you should wear. It's got purple gems, just like your hair."

I swing my glance back to Mackenzie, double-checking that she's up for this.

"You know this would include you meeting my Mum?" I ask, not wanting to deter her, but wanting her to know what she's getting into by agreeing to go.

She gives me a helpless shrug. She's in for the long haul, apparently.

"Then, I guess I'm meeting your mom."

I smooth my sweater, wishing I'd had time to change into something a bit more refined than jeans and a boot splattered with old mud. My leg brace doesn't add any flair to my appearance either. Maybe it was foolish of me to come here after all. The brace creaks as I shift my weight, tapping my fingers anxiously on my thigh.

"It'll be fine, you look beautiful as always," Ian murmurs, covering my hand gently with his own to still its nervous motion.

Hayley and June had conked out on the car ride here from Heathrow, miniature jet setters that they are. Now Ian lifts their slight, sleeping forms easily, our odd transatlantic menagerie trailing up the garden steps behind his broad back to face the 'monster' within.

Before we make it fully up the walk, the bright red door swings abruptly open. A petite woman with peppery blonde hair peers over us cooly. "Well, here you are at last..."

Ian immediately stiffens under her sweeping, silent criticism before letting a deep sigh escape him. Without warning he pivots slightly on the step below to face me directly, eyes earnest.

"Let's grab dinner around the corner after this. Just the two of us? I'd like that..." His gentle smile floods me with warmth against the sudden chill. "Right then, Mum," he says striding forward, "Allow me to introduce Mackenzie Roberts."

My palms grow slick, but my determination rises. If Ian can brave the fires, well, so can I.

"Nice to meet you, Mrs. Summer," I say boldly holding out one of my damp hands to shake hers. One thing I've learned in the music business is to never let them see you sweat. You might actually be sweating like a stuck pig, but never let it show that it's affecting you in any way. "I've heard a lot about you."

I leave that comment where it is for her to interpret as she likes. To be honest, what I've heard, I don't particularly care for. But as is the case with strangers you hear about before meeting, you don't know what you don't know. And I have no idea why Ian's mother ticks the way she does.

There are reasons for everything.

THE GIRLS ARE NAPPING IN THE GUEST ROOM, AND AN awkward silence hangs heavy as Mrs. Summer's assessing gaze rakes me up and down. I resist the urge to fidget under scrutiny, grasping mentally for any topic to cut the thick tension between all of us.

My eyes catch on a curio cabinet in the corner of the sitting room showcasing various animal figurines. I drift closer without thinking.

Is that a Lladró nautilus shell?

"These are exquisite," I breathe, leaning in to admire the meticulous sculpting of a sea turtle piece. "My mom used to collect these Spanish porcelain works when I was young. The craftsmanship is like none other."

I sense Ian's mom surveying this interaction from the doorway as I continue gently handling various figurines. The act reminds me painfully of times doing just this same thing with my own mother, marveling over new additions to her collection. A collection I now keep in my apartment.

Finally, Mrs. Summer clears her throat delicately. I glance over to see her features have softened marginally. "You have an eye for quality then," she acknowledges somewhat reluctantly. "Ian failed to mention your mother was also an admirer of fine arts."

I carefully set down a coral reef scene. "She had wonderful taste. I think she'd approve of your curation here. She gave me this ring," I say, stepping over to show her. "It's actually a heliconia flower, but she thought it looked like raven feathers, like the band, Murderous Crows, that I manage."

She arches an eyebrow as she takes my hand to examine the ring. I can't tell if she's really taking in the meaning behind it or checking for its authenticity. Surprisingly, she says, "It's lovely. And it does look like a row of bird feathers, doesn't it? How charming."

Behind me, Ian lets out an audible exhale. I quirk a faint, brief smile his way before turning my full charm back on the tougher audience member who I think is finally warming up. "I'd love it if you told me the story behind some of your pieces."

The battle is far from won, but perhaps the ice has cracked enough now for us to get to know one another.

I hover just outside the sitting room doorway, my pulse stilling as I take in the unbelievable sight before me. Mackenzie is laughing softly beside my mother over her Lladró collection that has been more shrine than decoration in this house for ages.

Mum has always treasured those sculptures, but God forbid grubby young hands like mine get anywhere near that crystal case when I was a boy. She rarely even handled them herself outside the occasional light dusting. Yet now, delicate coral reefs and flowers materialize gently in my taciturn mother's hands as she drinks in Mackenzie's admiration.

It's like peering through some portal to an alternate dimension. Ease and geniality have somehow replaced the arctic chill we both braced for on the way here. They truly bond over the figurines' craftsmanship and the stories behind certain purchases. Stories I've never heard before. But then, I never asked either, so that's on me.

Mackenzie's knowledge impresses Mum in return as she shares her own stories and those of her mother's collection. I shake my head slowly, the corner of my mouth quirking up. My spectacular girl, able to thaw even this Ice Queen.

When they finally notice my lingering presence, I raise my hands in mock surrender. "Apologies for interrupting rare artifact storytime." But my grin gives away to joy as Mackenzie's bright eyes meet mine from across the room. "I was just wondering about dinner?"

My mother tsks disapprovingly at me, "I thought I heard you say you were both going somewhere nearby for dinner alone?" I'd swear there's encouragement in her tone, but that can't be right.

"Well, I mean--" I start.

"No, no. Enough of this nonsense," My mother says, closing the door to the curio, and gently pressing Mackenzie in my direction. "You two go enjoy yourselves. I think the girls will be asleep for a while yet from the looks of it. We're not going anywhere."

"If you insist..." I demure, glancing at Mackenzie who can only shrug in response.

"Why don't you try the Shangri-La across the Thames? I hear their room service is quite tolerable."

Mackenzie's brows shoot up as she hears the term

'room service.' As do mine. Is she actually suggesting…?

"Go on you two," she insists, now pushing us both toward the front door. "Before I lose my good nature."

We both allow ourselves to be escorted out, coats handed to us roughly. And when the door shuts behind us, we turn to each other in disbelief.

"Did that just happen?" I ask, my warm breath pluming in the chilled air.

"I think it did," Mackenzie laughs, shrugging into her coat.

"Right then. Shangri-La?"

"Are you making the reservation, or am I?"

Maybe these two important pillars of my world, building unexpected bridges, shouldn't surprise me anymore. We've all been caught up in hidden depths lately. But witnessing stiff upper lips unpin themselves right before my eyes still feels a bit too miraculous.

THE SOUNDS OF LONDON TRAFFIC ALMOST IMPERCEPTIBLY float up from the streets below as I slide the keycard into our hotel room door. Mackenzie lingers just behind, uncharacteristically quiet since we left Mum's place. I chalk it up to surprise at the seismic shift with my mother's blessing over dinner, and whatever might come next for us alone. She's not the only one still surprised.

Flabbergasted, more like.

Inside, low lighting and a stupendous view of the Thames and London beyond bathe everything in a muted glow. This space feels suspended somewhere outside of real life, much like that snowy cabin hideaway where we first stumbled recklessly into each other. My heart starts to race remembering us wrapped in tangled sheets and Mackenzie's sly smile beckoning me toward ecstasy. I can't help but wonder what the next few hours might have in store for us.

I turn to find her hovering awkwardly as well near the entry table, clearly warring with herself. My brow furrows. Has she started second-guessing everything? I take a tentative step closer, ducking my head slightly to catch her amethyst eyes.

"Hey. No expectations here if it doesn't feel right yet," I murmur. Her tentative look wrenches my gut. We're navigating uncharted territory, but I swear to make it a safe passage regardless. "Maybe we can just see where things lead naturally?" I graze her wrist, feeling her unraveling tension.

A shaky laugh escapes her as she sways into my arms. We have time now, and trusting instincts got us this far.

But I absolutely have to know where this goes.

CHAPTER 53

OVER AND OVER AGAIN

MACKENZIE

I smile against Ian's comforting lips, the knot of awkwardness I felt earlier finally unfurls as his arms wrap solidly around me. Our mouths move slowly as if choreographing the first tentative steps of a dance we've almost forgotten.

I let my hands trail up his strong shoulders, thrilling as small shivers follow my touch. How many restless nights have there been since we last touched each other like this?

Too many.

My breath catches as Ian gently cups my neck, angling into a deeper kiss that instantly reignites the passion between us. Muscle memory kicks in, and we both know that one kiss is leading us further now. The decadent suite's dim lighting, and the romantic skyline view as a backdrop, fade into the periphery until only intoxicating sensory awareness of this man surrounds me.

I press closer into him with a soft noise of longing, sighing encouragement when clever hands trail teasingly down my sides in response. We may be moving cautiously as new partners after the seismic life shifts we're both experiencing, but I recognize and trust these timeless rhythms.

I recognize and trust *him*.

As Ian lifts my shirt, lips worshipping tenderly down my throat, I arch into him letting all of my last lingering doubts unravel.

"I was thinking I could really use a shower after the long flight..." I say suggestively, pulling his own shirt over his head.

"Yeah? Well, I...like the way you think," he says, swooping me into his arms, and carrying me into the room's attached én suite.

There are steps in the bathroom, leading up to a huge recessed bathtub the size of an Olympic swimming pool, with a view of the sun setting across the city skyline. It's breathtaking.

"Or, maybe a bath would be more relaxing?" Ian asks, already reaching over to start the water flowing.

I turn around to check the shower stall but see the colorful reflection of the orange and purple sky and turn quickly back. "Definitely a bath," I say, carefully removing my uncomfortable brace, and stripping off the rest of my clothes, as Ian does the same.

I barely have time to take in his exquisite form before the tub is full, and the smell of sweet lilacs from the bubbles fills the air.

"Here, I'll help you," Ian says, holding out a hand to help me up and into the steaming water. I instantly feel all of my muscles relax as he positions himself across from me, our legs tangling awkwardly at first, then making way for each other.

"Sorry. Sorry," he says, lifting my bad leg above the water to inspect the colorful bruises still mottling the skin on my calf. They've shifted in hue and aren't nearly as angry as they were right after the accident. "Looks as though it's healing up nicely, yeah?"

I nod. "Yup. It barely hurts anymore, either. That stupid brace is just for stability now."

"Good," he murmurs, laying a gentle kiss on my ankle before lowering my leg back into the water.

We fall into a relaxing quiet, steam rising all around us.

"This view is beautiful," I whisper, taking in the amazing colors of the sky.

"It is," he whispers back, and when I turn my head, I see he's looking at me with hooded eyes. Only me. Not the gorgeous sunset, or panoramic view of the city.

Me.

"Come here," he rasps, pulling me onto his lap. His erection presses against me, and a warmth grows low in my core, making my breath catch.

My body starts to move on its own, working my center along his length, torturing us both as our mouths crush together. Our breaths become ragged when we pull apart.

He rolls and twists the nipples of my breasts between expert fingers, sending jolts through me, only making me long to have him inside me once and for all. To ease this building tension that's been between us for days.

I reach to guide him inside me, to chase the sensation I know will push me over the edge like only he can. But, before going any further, Ian stops me, and glances up, pure passion in his eyes, but I sense hesitation, too. "You're sure?"

I was sure until he asked. Now his question makes me doubt myself. His hesitation makes me wonder if there's something else I don't know. Something I should know that would make him doubt this now.

Grabbing his face between my hands gently, I stare fiercely into his emerald eyes. There is nothing in this world that I want more than this man. "Swear to me that you aren't hiding anything else. Swear--"

"I swear it, Mackenzie," he says. "I swear it on my daughter's hearts. I'm not keeping anything else from you. I wouldn't dare."

I don't need to study his reaction to know he's telling the truth. I feel it in my soul.

Pulling him into a searing kiss seals our pact. We're taking this to the next level, and not just physically. The emotions flowing through both of us are evident with every scorching touch and every devouring kiss.

Once he slides inside me, I surrender to it all, groaning at his teasing with gentle thrusts.

Two can play this game, and I'm in control now.

Careful of my leg as I nestle around him, I lean back and grab his shoulders, gaining his attention. Our eyes meet with an intensity that only comes with deep emotion. Rotating my hips ever so slowly, I can't help the wicked smile that lifts the corners of my lips as his expression grows hungrier.

"Mackenzie..." he growls, leaning in to take a breast in his mouth, never breaking eye contact. I watch as his tongue swirls the stiff tip, then he nips it gently between his teeth. I can't help but twitch around him at the sight, and my movements quicken.

I start to rock up and down on his shaft, the hot water surrounding us only adds to the heat between us. Watching the droplets slide haphazardly down his neck as we create small waves, I lean in to lick one, its taste, mixed with the salt from his skin is delicious.

Ian takes advantage of the movement forward and plunges deep into me with a moan, pushing me over the edge I thought I was only getting close to. My orgasm erupts, and my entire body shudders as the furious pulsation between my legs peaks around him.

He mirrors my savage sounds as he explodes inside me, his body tensing and quivering under the water and beneath my hands. The vision of untethered ecstasy on his face as he comes down is beyond satis-fying. It's magical.

That two people can make each other feel so good is nothing less than a triumph. A miracle. I didn't know that sex could be this intimate. So soul binding.

And that's what we've done. We've bound our souls to one another. In a bathtub. In a strange hotel. Practically at his mother's insistence.

As fucked up as it sounds – it sounds about right for us.

Darkness cloaks the London streets as Mackenzie and I slide into the rental car, minds still swimming deliriously from a few coveted hours alone unraveling each other. The evening was a revelation after all of our recent turmoil. Naked vulnerability replaced both of our guarded hesitations at last.

The future now fills me with hope rather than doubt with this formidable woman willingly at my side. All secrets bared. Nothing more to come between us.

I brush my lips over Mackenzie's knuckles, memories replaying vividly. "I don't know that I deserve this rare second chance, but now that I have you, I'm not letting you go."

She flashes me that sly, knowing smile that first

sparked my fascination with her. "Remember that you said that when I'm hijacking your towels and stealing the covers at 3:00 a.m." Her eyes dance brighter than any sunrise. "But I suppose I'll keep you. For now, at least."

"THERE'S MY SLEEPYHEADS." I SWEEP HAYLEY INTO MY ARMS while June clings blearily to my leg, both fighting epic yawn battles. The treasured sight makes my chest swell. This reaction to my daughters is something I'll never get over. And I'll never hide it again. If anything comes from this relationship with Mackenzie, it's that. I have truly learned my lesson there.

I meet my mother's gaze over the girls' tousled bedheads, bracing for her usual complaint at my American life persisting. Instead, a gentle inquisitiveness lingers now. Her eyes flick curiously between a glowing Mackenzie and me.

"Seems dinner at the Shangri-La was pleasant after all?" Mum asks delicately as she passes Mackenzie the girls' glittered bags. There's no frosty judgment though, as I would have expected. Rather something resembling solidarity with the remarkable woman she's only just met seems to be brewing.

Mackenzie smiles easily, her stunning after-sex

radiance failing to escape Mum's notice if that probing look she's giving her is any indication.

"Yes, the hotel was really lovely. But I'm sad our visit here is almost over," Mackenzie says plainly, expertly avoiding my mum's innuendos.

Mum pats Mackenzie's hand fondly. "Oh nonsense, darling. This won't be the last. We've far too many artifact adventures ahead. I'm anxious to see your own collection." She pulls a surprised Mackenzie into a swift hug.

My mouth actually drops open in shock.

Somehow, a single day has removed decades of ingrained reserve from this matriarch of propriety.

I guess, if anyone could do it, it's Mackenzie. God bless her.

"Right then. Let's get this show on the road, shall we?" I say, letting my mother uncharacteristically peck my cheek.

Several rounds of therapy might be in order after this to sort through all these conflicting emotions now. I'm starting to feel something like whiplash from the changes happening all at once.

Hayley and June nod off again almost instantly after being buckled into the backseat for the short ride to Brianna's. I glance over to see Mackenzie in the passenger seat watching them fondly before turning my focus back to the road.

"So, on a scale of Arctic freeze to Chernobyl melt-down, how doomed am I about to be here with you meeting my ex?" I half-joke.

Mackenzie arches an eyebrow. "Surely you're joking. I wrangle rockstars for a living. Remember?"

I have to laugh even as anxiety creeps higher nearing Brianna's neighborhood. "Well, don't say I didn't warn you about Hurricane Brianna..."

We've barely rolled to a stop before the imposing front door is thrown open, and the lady of the manor glides out with far more grace than the occasion calls for. I unconsciously flex my scarred hand seeing Brianna's familiar beauty queen facade slide into place.

Not surprisingly, Axel is now nowhere to be seen. He must have outlived his usefulness to Bri. Or maybe he needed to practice his lip-syncing skills and dance moves. One of the two.

"Back so soon, Ian?" she asks sharply, assuming an air of superiority she doesn't own. And it's bullshit anyway. She knew the girls were coming home this evening.

I open my mouth to respond but Hayley pops up sleepy-eyed first. "Mummy, Kenzie reads the best stories." June also wakes and smiles shyly at Mackenzie.

At that, Brianna's shrewd gaze cuts to Mackenzie

hanging back politely. I tense, cursing myself for not prepping her for this particular brand of toxic femininity.

"And you must be Kenzie?" Her tone drips icicles, her frozen smile never wavering.

I clear my throat, bristling, but Mackenzie beats me to cordial introductions unfazed.

"I am. Nice to meet you," she says, putting on her manager voice, and shaking Brianna's reluctant hand. "Your daughters are the best. I really enjoyed spending time with them."

Still, my girls are oblivious to the animosity simmering beneath their mother's façade, but I see it plain as day.

Brianna's frozen hospitality melts instantly to a frown before she recovers her plasticized features. "Thank you," she says, her voice now stilted.

She's met her match, I'd say.

Regardless of how Brianna reacts or doesn't to Mackenzie, the girls' joy over her now in our lives tells me everything I need to know about our newly blended souls: This foundation won't crack from a passing storm.

Not if I have anything to say about it.

THE PLANE LEVELED OUT ABOVE THE CLOUDS A WHILE AGO, and beside me Mackenzie's breath deepens into sleep, her head resting heavy on my shoulder. A few messy purple strands tickle where they escape her braids until I gently brush them back. Even exhausted she still takes my freaking breath away. Her beauty is somehow both fiercer and softer now that I know the full force of her passionate heart.

I watch the dark clouds scroll by through the tiny window, my leg jiggling restlessly with excess energy. So much has snapped into dizzying focus these past few weeks. Everything building up, shattering apart, and then somehow realigning into perfection.

It felt like a fucking bullet ricocheting from my mum's to Brianna's households today. Their opposite reactions to the woman sleeping here, blissfully unaware of my racing brain.

But maybe it's good the seismic shifts keep coming. They forced me to own my dishonesty, then fight like hell through the shitty aftermath. And somehow, I lucked into gaining so much in return. This feisty new partner challenging and supporting me, understanding and accepting all of my flaws. And my girls...God, they already adore her.

How could they not?

I know I do.

We are heading towards a hectic life. Surviving in the music industry isn't easy on the best days, and to do it with someone like Mackenzie as a partner makes it all feel doable somehow. Even the relationship we're building. That's something I never expected. Something I never saw coming.

I find for once I'm not overthinking the future. In fact, I'm anxious to get there. Because here, tucked against my side, rests the only sure path ahead worth taking. Bumpy patches be damned, for once my guiding light now shines clear as day.

And I will never do anything to jeopardize that again.

Ever.

Turbulence shakes the plane, and Mackenzie stirs, eyes bleary as she looks around. "Are we there yet?"

I caress her cheek, "No, love. Just some turbulence. Go back to sleep."

She stretches with a yawn and lays her head back onto my shoulder. "I'm not sleepy."

"Oh, okay then," I chuckle, knowing she's dead tired.

"Tell me a story," she says, nuzzling into my neck, her breath warm in the cool air of the plane.

"How about a question?"

She hugs my arm tighter. "What kind of question?"

"If..."

"Oh boy, here we go."

"If a man is in love, like brutally, heartbreakingly in love, with someone he knows he doesn't deserve, should he tell her?"

She's silent and her body freezes at the question.

Snapping her gaze up to me, she searches my eyes intensely. Looking for the lie I know isn't there.

"It's me, Mackenzie. I'm the man in love...with you."

Her entire being changes, and she softens somehow, all of her hard edges blurring as my words sink in.

"I love you, too, Ian."

And with that, my whole life changes. *Our* lives change. And I won't fight it anymore. I can't.

Screw going back in time, I want to see where this goes.

Note to self in the fresh mental notebook: Readjust the time machine coordinates to the amazing future ahead of us.

All of us.

"Alright boys, let's get this murder started!" I announce brightly, eliciting the expected round of groans as the band piles into our rehearsal space. Another year, another strategy session to map the chaotic road ahead. But for once, my optimism seems to outpace the anxiety I carried into last year.

I gaze fondly around the circle of familiar faces. Most of them constants after a decade together now post-tragedy and triumph. We came perilously close to splintering for good when Andy's senseless drunk driving death sent shockwaves through our tight-knit musical family. I honestly didn't think Jake would recover from that, but since he and Cassidy got together, he's been nothing but solid.

Then, when we found Skyler to replace Andy,

things changed for all of us again. Especially for Logan who found his long-lost soulmate in her. Watching them connect, or reconnect, as it were, was inspiring. And it never gets in the way of the band or the music. And now with them married, it almost seems even more meant to be than it ever was.

Cooper's recovery from being labeled a 'bad boy' to now earnestly in love with his fiancée Sloane after meeting at the music program he tutored has been a transformation I never saw coming. He was a particular target of the late Nyx's media assault on the band, but he came out the other side of it better than ever. Out of everyone, I never saw Cooper settling down. And yet, I think he might be next in line to make their wedding official. I know Sloane's been busy making the arrangements in between her own blossoming music career, and continued work at the music foundation.

Remy's love story might be my favorite, though it was painful to witness firsthand. He fell so hard for Monroe who, at first, couldn't take the pressure that being in a relationship with a rockstar requires. But somewhere off in Italy she found a way within herself to deal with it and has happily put Remy out of his stupid misery without her.

Man, he was so fucking miserable to live with for a long time.

These people are like brothers and a sister to me.

And despite the bullshit they've put me through over the years, I wouldn't trade them for the world.

The cell next to me buzzes with Ian's incoming support text for conquering this yearly meeting.

IAN: Go get 'em, tiger. :D

And there's my own soulmate. My unsuspecting hero. My lips quirk remembering the frigid day I first barreled into his world on those stupid skis...

God, I love him.

"Earth to fearless leader..." Jake teases in his smooth voice. I flick a spare guitar pick at him without malice. We've braved much worse than meetings planning tours and singles.

As long as we cling to this bond, our musical parade marches on, stronger for the storms we've weathered together. Tragedy struck cruel blows, but this year's sunlight already glints promisingly through the clouds drifting past us.

I get up, and hold my arm out, palm down. "Okay, c'mon. You assholes know the drill." I stifle the smirk, playing on my lips as they each pull themselves up and over to me.

Logan and Skyler put their hands on top of mine first, wedding rings glistening and giving each other affectionate looks. Remy and Cooper eye each other with smiles as they do the same.

Jake steps up, but hesitates, looking at each of us in

turn without a word, but nodding to himself thought-fully before placing his hand on top of the pile.

The crow tattoos on each of our hands now nested.

"Let's do this, fam," he says solemnly.

"Murderous Crows, mates for life!"

--THE END—

SUSTAIN PLAYLIST

Spotify: https://open.spotify.com/playlist/5AXXhj3oO5omSFt05lvBSe?si=dd08d1792e55451c
YouTube: https://www.youtube.com/playlist?list=PLafab1Kmq5pYAXYGqphL42iU4YgNl9TNp

1. The Pretty Reckless, Death By Rock and Roll
2. 10 Years, *The Optimist*
3. Ava Max, *Cold as Ice*
4. Nothing But Thieves, *Emergency*
5. Diamante, *Ghost Myself*
6. Grant Lee Buffalo, *Honey Don't Think*
7. Spyres, *Otherside*
8. Spyres, *Fix You*
9. Stand Atlantic, *Toothpick*
10. The Ninth Wave, *Hard Not to Hold You*
11. Emily Jane White, *Hands*

12. Hoobastank, *Head Over Heels*
13. Taylor Swift, Fall Out Boy, *Electric Touch*
14. Hozier, *Like Real People Do*
15. Bea Miller, *Lonely Bitch*
16. The Pale White, *Confession Box*
17. Sam Phillips, *What Do I Do*
18. Wind Walkers, *Dead Talk*
19. Aeseaes, *Carrion Comfort*
20. Des Rocs, *Hanging By A Thread*
21. Lucia & The Best Boys, *So Sweet I Could Die*
22. Roxy Music, *More Than This*
23. Silk City, Dua Lipa, Diplo, Mark Ronson, *Electricity*
24. Fame on Fire, *Plastic Heart*
25. Gavin Mikhail, The Cameron Collective, *In The Name Of Love*
26. Placebo, *The Bitter End*
27. PJ Harvey, *One Line*
28. Chri$tian Gate$, *Traumatized*
29. Plush, *Find the Beautiful*
30. Fame on Fire, Ice Nine Kills, *Welcome to the Chaos*
31. Nita Strauss, Dorothy, *Victorious*
32. Thousand Foot Krutch, *Light Up the Sky*
33. Halestorm, *The Steeple*
34. Seether, *Against the Wall*
35. Natalie Taylor, *Surrender*
36. Caskets, *Guiding Light*
37. Sofia Karlberg, *Crazy in Love*

38. Grant Lee Buffalo, *Mockingbirds*
39. Wolf Alice, *Don't Delete the Kisses*
40. Arcane Roots, *Half the World*
41. Seafret, *Oceans*
42. Little Image, *Out of My Mind*
43. The Knife, *Heartbeats*
44. Atreyu, *Drowning*
45. The Bangles, *Hero Takes A Fall*
46. Catch Your Breath, *Yesterday*
47. Hozier, *Francesca*
48. Foo Fighters, *Miracle*
49. Verite, *By Now*
50. Depeche Mode, *World In My Eyes*
51. Halestorm, *Strange Girl*
52. John Lennon, *Oh My Love*
53. Nathan Sykes, Ariana Grande, *Over and Over Again*
54. Civil Twilight, *Next To Me*
55. Thousand Foot Krutch, *We Are*

SERIES
ACKNOWLEDGMENTS

First and foremost, thank you readers for taking this wild ride with me. Your words of encouragement and love of my writing make this all worthwhile. The emotional rollercoaster that has been writing this particular series was difficult to get through at times, and I couldn't have done it without you.

This includes all of my ARC/ALC readers – you guys are really the rockstars here. Don't worry – I know it.

Second – all my friends (you know who you are) who know to leave me alone while I'm writing. Yes, I've missed a lot of things, but you understand how important this whole writing deal is to me. Our love language has always been space, and know that it's recognized and put to good use. My weird, introverted heart loves you all.

Third, all the pros that I've worked with on this series, from the cover photos (all but this last one) Wander Aguiar, my magnificent editor/beta reader Cal LaBorde - @calreads1310, proofreading on a few by Chloe Trivelpiece - @Bibliophile_Chloe, and, of course, the narrators that brought books one and two to life so far – Samantha Brentmoor, Aaron Shedlock, Kit Swann, and Blake Lockheart. (I do still hope to get the rest on audio!)

A couple of things to mention for this particular book:

The *If* books are real! And, I highly recommend them. There are four books total, and the one I referenced in *Sustain* is *If³...(citation below),* and is available just about everywhere. Check them out.

McFarlane, Evelyn, and James Saywell. *If³...(Questions for the Game of Love)*. Villard Books, ©1997.

If you're wondering where the crazy name 'Corpse Limousine' came from – thank my sister, who helped when I couldn't think of the word for hearse...Writing is exactly that random sometimes.

Finally, it's my real life that gives me experiences to draw from to ground these stories in some sort of real-ity. It's not always pretty and is often painful. Sometimes even downright devastating. I'm hopefully a stronger person now because of them. For that much, at least, I'm grateful.

If any of these books made you laugh, cry, rage, or smile, just know that I did the exact same when I lived it, and when wrote it.

If you enjoyed this book, please consider taking a moment to leave a Review. Even a star rating helps indie authors reach a wider audience.

goodreads   amazon kindle   BookBub

Also by Amy Booker

Near Miss Rock Star Series

Almost

So Close

Barely

Near Miss Rock Star Collection

In Reach

Drive Me Wild Vegas Series

Ms. Fortune

Ms. Chief

Ms. Lead

Ms. Take

The Mischief Motors Collection

Rhapsody Rock Star Series

Coda

Reprise

Overture

Waltz

Sustain

Chaos Fuel Rock Star Series

Mayhem

CONTACT AMY

FOLLOW

My website: http://www.amybookerauthor.com
Facebook: www.facebook.com/amybookerauthor
Instagram: www.instagram.com/amy_booker_author/
TikTok: www.TikTok.com/@amybookerauthor
Goodreads: www.goodreads.com/author/show/
22225202.Amy_Booker
Amazon: https://rebrand.ly/sraegoj

BUY DIRECT

Amy Booker Store: https://payhip.com/AmyBooker

INTERACT

Email: amybookerauthor@gmail.com
Facebook Reader Group: https://www.facebook.com/
groups/amybookersroadies
Newsletter Sign Up: https://www.amybookerauthor.
com/subscribe

READ EARLY

Join my ARC Team: https://forms.
gle/Ns1QKmrrsQz4ay5S6